World Famous Authors & Poets

Dr. Gagan Jain, *D.Litt.*

MGB®

NEW DELHI (INDIA)

World Famous Authors & Poets

This English Edition, Published in India

Published by

MG BOOKS

An Imprint of

MAANU GRAPHICS

MAANU GRAPHICS
(PUBLISHERS OF GENERAL BOOKS)
5FF, Ganpati Bhawan, 21 Ansari Road,
Darya Ganj, New Delhi-110002
Ph: 43755225, 9315898404
E-mail : maanugraphics@yahoo.com
mgbooks.maanu@yahoo.com

Printed at
Satyam Enterprises, Delhi

CONTENTS

ABOUT THE BOOK

World Famous Authors and Poets, authored by Gagan Jain, is a captivating book that takes readers on an enthralling journey through the lives and works of some of the greatest literary figures in history.

From renowned authors who have shaped the landscape of literature to revered poets whose verses have touched the hearts of millions, this book offers a comprehensive exploration of their lives, literary contributions, and the enduring impact they have had on the world of literature.

World Famous Authors and Poets, penned by Gagan Jain, offers an immersive journey through the annals of literary excellence.

By delving into the lives, works, and impact of famous authors and poets, the book provides readers with a comprehensive understanding of the evolution of literature throughout history.

From the pioneers who laid the groundwork to the contemporary voices shaping the literary world, this book celebrates the power of words and the enduring influence of these literary giants.

Whether you are a seasoned literature enthusiast or a curious newcomer, this book promises to inspire, educate, and captivate readers of all backgrounds.

AGATHA CHRISTIE

Agatha Christie (1890-). Except for Georges Simenon, Agatha Christie is the only writer of fiction whose works have sold over 300 million copies throughout the world. In the United Kingdom alone, just the paper-back editions of her books sell over 1.5 million copies a year. And her singular triumphs are not confined to the world of books. Her play The Mousetrap has enjoyed the longest continuous run of any show at one theater. On November 25, 1952, this melodrama opened at the Ambassadors Theatre in London, and it broke the record on February 28, 1972, with its 8,000th performance. Next to Shakespeare, Agatha Christie is the 2nd most-translated English author.

These staggering achievements have been made by a generally retiring woman who gets her best ideas while eating apples in her bathtub. Agatha Christie was born in Torquay, Devon, England. Her father, Frederick Alvah Miller of New York, died when she was very young, and she was reared by her mother and educated privately. It was her mother who encouraged her writing.

One day young Agatha had a cold and could not go out. Her mother suggested that she amuse herself by writing a story. Later, she studied singing in Paris but was disappointed when she realized that her voice was not of star quality. To console herself Agatha Christie wrote a novel, which she showed to a literary neighbor, and he encouraged her to continue her efforts.

From time to time she was fortunate enough to have a short story published. However, her 1st great success did not come until after her marriage to an English army officer, Archibald Christie. While he was away fighting in W.W. I, she wrote a detective novel in her free time away from her work as a volunteer nurse. After many rejections, it was finally published in 1920 under the title The Mysterious Affair at Styles.

The book was a success, and it introduced one of the greatest fictional sleuths of all time, Hercule Poirot, a worthy successor to Sherlock Holmes. Like Holmes, Poirot relies not on gimmickry but on what he calls the "little gray cells" to solve the crime. This clever Belgian is matched by Miss Jane Marple, another Christie creation, who deftly spots murderers by drawing on her knowledge of the people in her own small English village. People are the same everywhere, she says, and it is best to suspect the worst of everyone in a murder case.

In real life Agatha Christie herself was once the subject of a mystery. She disappeared from her home in December, 1926, and a nationwide search was launched for her. An anonymous letter brought her searchers to a hotel where they found her suffering from amnesia and living under the name of the woman who was to become her husband's 2nd wife. After her divorce, she subsequently met and married Max Mallowan, an archaeologist, whom she has accompanied on his expeditions to Egypt and the Near East. These excursions have often provided backgrounds for her novels.

Now in her middle 80s, she still writes at least one novel a year, adding to a total that matches her age. Her works offer murder in pleasant surroundings. She emphasizes plot and character and eschews violence for its own sake. Among her greatest triumphs are The Murder of Roger Ackroyd, a tale that brilliantly defied all the canons of detective fiction, and Ten Little Indians, also published as And Then There Were None. To the public and critics alike, she remains the world's greatest mystery writer.

ALEXANDRE DUMAS

Alexandre Dumas, père, (1802-1870) was one of the most famous French writers of the 19th century. Dumas is best known for historical adventure novels like *The Three Musketeers* and *The Count of Monte Cristo*, both written within the space of two years, 1844-45, and which belong to the foundation works of popular culture. He was among the first, along with Honoré de Balzac and Eugène Sue, who fully used the possibilities of roman feuilleton, the serial novel.

Dumas is credited with revitalizing the historical novel in France, although his abilities as a writer were under dispute from the beginning. Dumas' works are fast-paced adventure tales that blend history and fiction, but on the other hand, the are entangled, melodramatic, and actually not faithful to the historical facts.

Alexandre Dumas was born in Villes-Cotterêts. His grandfather was a French nobleman, who had settled in Santo Domingo (now part of Haiti); his paternal grandmother, Marie-Cessette, was an Afro-Caribbean, who had been a black slave in the French colony (now part of Haiti). Dumas's father was a general in Napoleon's army, who had fallen out of favor. After his death in 1806 the family lived in poverty.

Dumas worked as a notary's clerk and went in 1823 to Paris to find work. Due to his elegant handwriting he secured a position with the Duc d'Orléans — later King Louis Philippe. He also found his place in theater and as a publisher of some obscure magazines. An illegitimate son called Alexandre Dumas fils, whose mother, Marie-Catherine Labay, was a dressmaker, was born in 1824.

As a playwright Dumas made his breakthrough with "Henri III et Sa Cour" (1829), produced by the Comedie Francaise. It gained a huge success and Dumas went on to write additional plays, of which "La Tour de Nesle" (1832, "The Tower of Nesle") is considered the greatest masterpiece of French melodrama. He wrote constantly, producing a steady stream of plays, novels, and short stories.

Historical novels brought Dumas enormous fortune, but he could spent money faster than he made it. He produced some 250 books with his 73 assistants, especially with the history teacher Auguste Maquet, whom he wisely allowed to work quite independently. Dumas earned roughly 200,000 francs yearly and received an annual sum of 63,000 francs for 220,000 lines from the newspapers Presse and the Constitutionel.

Maquet often proposed subjects and wrote first drafts for some of Dumas' most famous serial novels, including *Les Trois Mousquetaires* (1844, *The Three Musketeers*) and *Le Comte de Monte-Cristo* (1844-45, *The Count of Monte-Cristo*). As a master dialogist, Dumas developed character traits, and kept the action moving, and composed the all-important chapter endings - teaser scenes that maintained suspense and readers interest to read more.

Dumas' role in the development of the historical novel owes much to a coincidence. The lifting of press censorship in the 1830s gave rise to a rapid spread of newspapers. Editors began to lure readers by entertaining serial novels. Everybody read them, the aristocracy, and the bourgeoisie, young and old, men and women. Dumas' first true serial novel was *Le Capitaine Paul* (1838, *Captain Paul*), a quick rewrite of a play.

Dumas lived as adventurously as the heroes of his books. He took part in the revolution of July 1830, caught cholera during the epidemic of 1832, and traveled in Italy to recuperate. He married his mistress Ida Ferrier, an actress, in 1840, but he soon separated after having spent her entire dowry. With the money earned from his writings, he built a fantastic Château Monte cristo on the outskirts of Paris.

In 1851 Dumas escaped his creditors - his country house, the Chateau de Monte Cristo. Dumas spent two years in exile in Brussels (1855-57), and then returned to Paris. In 1858 he traveled to Russia and in1860 he went to Italy, where he supported Garibaldi and Italy's struggle for independence (1860-64). He then remained in Naples as a keeper of the museums for four years. After his return to France his debts continued to mount.

Called as "the king of Paris", Dumas earned fortunes and spent them right away on friends, art, and mistresses. Dumas died of a stroke on December 5, 1870, at Puys, near Dieppe. His son Alexandre Dumas fils, became a writer, dramatist, and moralist, who never accepted his father's lifestyle.

Dumas did not generally define himself as a black man, and there is not much evidence that he encountered overt racism during his life. However, his works were popular among the 19th-century African-Americans, partly because in *The Count of Monte-Cristo*, the falsely imprisoned Edmond Dantès, may be read as a parable of emancipation. In a shorter work, *Georges* (1843, *George*), Dumas examined the question of race and colonialism. The main character, a half-French mulatto, leaves Mauritius to be educated in France, and returns to avenge himself for the affronts he had suffered as a boy.

ANTON CHEKHOV

Russian playwright, one of the great masters of modern short story. In his work Chekhov combined the dispassionate attitude of a scientist and a doctor with the sensitivity and psychological understanding of an artist. Chekhov portrayed often life in the Russian small towns, where tragic events occur in a minor key, as a part of everyday life. His characters are passive, filled with the feeling of hopelessness and the fruitlessness of all efforts. "What difference does it make?" says Chebutykin in *Three Sisters.*

Anton Chekhov was born in Taganrog, Ukraine, as the son of a grocer and grandson of a serf who had bought his freedom in 1841. His mother was Yevgenia Morozov, the daughter of a cloth merchant. Chekhov's childhood was shadowed by his father's tyranny and religious fanaticism.

He attended a school for Greek boys in Taganrog (1867-68) and Taganrog grammar school (1868-79). The family was forced to move to Moscow following his father's bankruptcy. At the age of 16 Chekhov became independent and remained for some time alone in his native town, supporting himself through private tutoring.

In 1879 Chekhov entered the Moscow University Medical School. While in the school he started to publish hundreds of comic short stories to support himself and his mother, sisters and brothers.

By 1886 he had gained wide fame as a writer. Chekhov published his works in St. Petersburg daily papers, *Peterburskaia gazeta* from 1885, and *Novoe vremia* from 1886. He also published two full-length novels of which *The Shooting Party* was translated into English in 1926.

Chekhov graduated in 1884, and practiced medicine until 1892. In 1886 Chekhov met H.S. Suvorin, who invited him to become a regular contributor for the St. Petersburg daily *Novoe vremya*. His friendship with Suvorin ended in 1898 because of his objections to the anti-Dreyfus campaingn conducted by the daily. But during these years Chechov developed his concept of the dispassionate, non-judgemental author.

He outlined his program in a letter to his brother Aleksandr: *"1. Absence of lengthy verbiage of political-social-economic nature; 2. total objectivity; 3. truthful descriptions of persons and objects; 4. extreme brevity; 5. audacity and originality; flee the stereotype; 6.*

compassion." Chechov's refusal to join the ranks of social critics arose the wrath of liberal and radical intellitentsia and he was criticized for avoidance of offering solutions to his serious social and moral themes. However, he was defended by such leading writers as Leo Tolstoy and Nikolai Leskov.

The failure of his play *The Wood Demon* (1889) and problems with his novel made Chekhov to withdraw from literature for a period. In 1890 he travelled across Siberia to remote Island, Sakhalin, where he conducted a detailed census of some 10 000 convicts and settlers condemned to live their lives on that harsh island. Chechov hoped to use the results of his research for his doctoral dissertation.

From this journey was born his famous travel book *The Island: A Journey to Sakhalin* (1893-94). Chekhov returned to Russia via Singapore, India, Ceylon, and the Suez Canal. From 1892 to 1899 Chekhov worked in Melikhovo, and in Yalta from 1899. Chekhov's fist book of stories (1886) was a success, and gradually he became a full-time writer.

Chekhov was awarded the Pushkin Prize in 1888. In 1889 he was elected a member of the Society of Lovers of Russian Literature. In 1900 he became a member of the Academy of Sciences in St. Petersburg, but resigned his membership two years later as a protest against the cancellation by the authorities of Gorky's election to the Academy. Later, in 1900, Gorky wrote to him: *"After any of your stories, however insignificant, everything appears crude, as if written not by a pen, but by a cudgel."*

Although Chekhov wrote several hundred stories, his fame today rests primarily on his plays. Chekhov used ordinary conversations, pauses, noncommunication, nonhappening, incomplete thoughts, to reveal the truth behind trivial words and daily life.

His characters belong often to the provincial middle class, petty aristocracy or landowners of prerevolutionary Russia. They contemplate their unsatisfactory lives unable to make decisions and help themselves when a crisis breaks out.

Chekhov's first full-length plays were failures. When *The Seagull* was revised in 1898 by Stanislavsky at the Moscow Art Theatre, he gained also fame as a playwright.

Among his masterpieces from this period is *Uncle Vanya* (1900), a melancholic story of Sonia and his brother-in-law Ivan (Uncle Vanya) who see their dreams and hopes passing in drudgery for others.

The Three Sisters (1901) was set in a provincial garrison town. The talented Prozorov sisters, whose hopes have much in common with the Brontë sisters, recognize the uselessness of their lives and cling to one another for consolation.

In *The Cherry Orchaid* (1904) reflected the larger developments in the Russian society. Mme Ranevskaias returns to her estate and finds out that the family house, together with the adjoining orchard, is to be auctioned.

Her brother Gaev is too impractical to help in the crisis. The businessman Lopakhin purchases the estate and the orchard is demolished. *"Everything on earth must come to an end..."*

In these three famous plays Chekhov blended laughter and tears, leaving much room for imagination - his plays like stories reflect a multitude of possible viewpoints.

Usually in Chekhov's dramas surprise and tension are not key elements, the dramatic movement is subdued, his characters do not fight, they endure their fate with patience.

In 1892 Chekhov bought a country estate in the village of Melikhove, where his best stories were written, including '*Neighbours*' (1892), '*Ward Number Six*' (1892), '*The Black Monk*' (1894), '*The Murder*' (1895), and '*Ariadne*' (1895).

He also served as a volunteer census taker, participated in famine relief, and worked as a medical inspector during cholore epidemics. In 1897 he fell ill with tuberculosis and lived since either abroad or in the Crimea. In Yalta he wrote his famous stories '*The Man in a Shell*,' '*Gooseberries*,' '*About Love*,' '*Lady with the Dog*,' and '*In the Ravine*.'

His last great story, '*The Betrothed*,' was an optimistic tale of a young woman who escapes from provincial dullness into personal freedom. In 1901 he married the Moscow Art Theater actress Olga Knipper (1870-1959), who had on stage several years central roles in his plays. Chekhov died on July 14/15, 1904, in Badenweiler, Germany. He was buried in the cemetery of the Novodeviche Monastery in Moscow.

Though a celebrated figure by the Russian literary public at the time of his death, Chekhov remained rather unknown internationally until the years after World War I, when his works were translated into English.

BANKIM CHANDRA CHATTERJEE

Bankim Chandra Chatterjee was born in the village Kanthalpura, the youngest of three brothers, to Yadav (or Jadab) Chandra Chattopadhyaya andDurgadebi. His family was orthodox, and his father, a government official, went on to become the Deputy Collector of Midnapur. He was educated at the Mohsin College in Hooghly and later at the Presidency College, graduating with a degree in Arts in 1857. He was one of the first two graduates of the Calcutta University.

Later, in 1869, he obtained a degree in Law as well. He was the author of *Vande Mataram* or *Bande Mataram* that inspired the freedom fighters of India, and was later declared the National Song of India. He did for Bengali fiction what Michael Madhusudan Dutt had done for Bengali poetry, that is, he brought in imagination. Chatterjee was more fortunate than Dutt as he did not have to set up his own diction from the very start. The prose style was already standardized; what Chatterjee did was to break its monotony, shear off its ponderous verbosity and give it a twist of informality and intimacy. Chatterjee's own style grew up as he went on writing.

Chatterjee, following the discipline of Isvarchandra Gupta, began his literary career as a writer of verse. Fortunately he was not slow to feel that poetry was not his metier. He then turned to fiction. His first attempt was a novel in Bengali submitted for a declared prize. The prize did not come to him and the novelette was never published. His first fiction to appear in print was Rajmohan's Wife. It was written in English and was probably a translation of the novelette submitted for the prize.

Durgeshnandini, his first Bengali romance, was published in 1865. The next novel Kapalkundala(1866) is one of the best romances written by Chatterjee. The theme is lyrical and gripping and, in spite of the melodrama and the dual story, the execution is skillful. the heroine, named after the mendicant woman in Bhavabhuti's Malatimadhava , is modelled partly after Kalidasa's Sakuntala and partly after Shakespeare's Miranda.

The next romance Mrinalini(1869) indicates an ameturishness and a definite falling off from the standard. It is a love romance against a historical background sadly neglected and confused. After this Chatterjee was not content to continue only as a writer of prose romances, but appeared also as a writer with the definite mission of simulating the intellect of the Bengali speaking people through literary campaign and of bringing about a cultural revival thereby. With this end in view he brought out monthly Bangadarshan in 1872. In the pages of this magazine all his writings except the very last two works first came out. These writings include novels, stories, humorous sketches, historical and miscellaneous essays, informative articles, religious discourses, literary criticisms and reviews. Vishbriksha (The poison Tree, 1873) was his first novel to appear serially in Bangadarshan.

Chandrasekhar (1877) suffers markedly from the impact of two parallel plots which have little common ground. The scene is once shifted back to eighteenth century. But the novel is not historical. The plot has suffered from the author's weakness for the occult. The next novel Rajani(1877) followed the autobiographical technique of Wilkie Collins' A Woman in White. The title role was modelled after Bulwar Lytton's Nydia in Last Days of Pompeii. In this romance of a blind girl, Chatterjee is at his best as a literary artist. In Krishnakanter Uil (Krishnakanta's Will, 1878) Chatterjee added some amount of feeling to imagination, and as a result it approaches nearest to the western novel.

The only novel of Chatterjee's that can claim full recognition as historical fiction is Rajsimha (1881, rewritten and enlarged 1893). Anandamath (The mission house of the Anandas, 1882) is a political novel without a sufficient plot. It definitely marks the decline of Chatterjee's power as a novelist. The plot of the meagre story is based on the Sannyasi rebellion that occurred in North Bengal in 1773. As fiction it can not be called an outstanding work.

But as the book that interpreted and illustrated the gospel of patriotism and gave Bengal the song "Vande Mataram" (I worship mother) which became the mantra of nationalism and the national song. Incidentally it gave tremendous impetus to the various patriotic and national activities culminating in the terrorist movement initiated in Bengal in the first decade of the twentieth century.

Devi Caudhurani by Chatterjee was published in 1884. The story is romantic and interesting and delightfully told, no doubt. Chatterjee's last novel Sitaram (1886) has for its theme the insurgence of a Hindu chief of lower central Bengal against the impotent Muslim rule. The central figure is well delineated but the other figures are either too idealistic or impalpable.

After the novels, the humorous sketches are the outstanding productions of Chatterjee. Kamalakanter Daptar (The Scribbling of Kamalakanta, 1875; enlarged as Kamalakanta, 1885) contains half humorous and half serious sketches somewhat after De Quincey's Confessions of an English Opium-eater. It shows the writer at his best.

Bankim Chatterjee was superb story-teller, and a master of romance. He is also a great novelist in spite of the fact that his outlook on life was neither deep nor critical, nor was his canvas wide. But he was something more than a great novelist. He was a path finder and a path maker. Chatterjee represented the English-educated Bengalee with a tolerably peaceful home life, sufficient wherewithal and some prestige, as the bearer of the torch of western enlightment. No Bengali writer before or since has enjoyed such spontaneous and universal popularity as Chatterjee. His novels have been translated in almost all the major languages of India, and have helped to simulate literary impulses in those languages. Bankim Chandra Chatterjee passed away on April 8, 1894.

BRAM STOKER

Abraham (Bram) Stoker was born November 8, 1847 at 15 The Crescent, Clontarf, North of Dublin, the third of seven children. For the first 7 years of his life Stoker was bedridden with a myriad of childhood diseases which afforded him much time to reading. By the time he went to college, Stoker had somehow overcome his childhood maladies and while at Trinity College, Dublin, the honor student was involved in soccer and was a marathon running champion. He was also involved in various literary and dramatic activities, a precursor to his later interests in the theater and his involvement with the rising action Henry Irving, whose performance he had critiqued as a student at Trinity. After graduation from college, and in his father's footsteps, he became a civil servant, holding the position of junior clerk in the Dublin Castle.

His literary career began as early as 1871 and in that year he took up a post as the unpaid drama critic for the "Evening Mail," while at the same time writing short stories. His first literary "success" came a year later when, in 1872, The London Society published his short story "The Crystal Cup." As early as 1875 Stoker's unique brand of fiction had come to the forefront. In a four part serial called the "Chain of Destiny," were themes that would become Stoker's trademark: horror mixed with romance, nightmares and curses.

Stoker encountered Henry Irving again, this time in the role of Hamlet, 10 years after Stoker's Trinity days. Stoker, still very much the critic (and still holding his civil service position), gave Irving's performance a favorable review. Impressed with Stoker's review, Irving invited Stoker back stage and the resultant friendship lasted until Irving's death in 1905.

The Stoker/Irving partnership solidified around the year 1878. During this time Henry Irving had taken over his own theater company called the London Lyceum, but he didn't like the management, and therefore approached Stoker to handle business, at which point Stoker gave up his government job and became the acting manager of the theater. A short time after Stoker began his new career, the publishing house of Sampson, Lowe contacted him expressing interest in a collection of Stoker's stories.

"Under the Sunset" was published in 1891 and was well received by some of the critics, but others thought the book too terrifying for children. Stoker was already fascinated with the notion of the "boundaries of life and death" which made this book too terrifying for children at least in some of the reviewer's minds. By the time Stoker had received favorable reviews for his romance novel "The Snake's Pass" (1890), he was already making notes for a novel with a vampire theme, and by 1894 he was back to macabre themes. It seemed only a natural consequence that "Dracula" would follow and was published in June 1897. Reviews on "Dracula" were mixed, and the book never yielded much money for Stoker. In a favorable review the "Daily Mail" compared it with "Frankenstein" and Poe's "The Fall of the House of Usher." "The Bookman" found it likeable in spots but commented that the "descriptions were hideous and repulsive."

For the next few years after "Dracula's" publication, events took a downward spiral for both Irving and Stoker. There were troubles with Irving's establishment and a fire destroyed part of the theater (including some important scenery) and Irving eventually sold it. Stoker did manage however to publish "The Jewel of the 7 Stars" in 1903, and it was a novel based on the information given to Stoker by an Egyptologist. In 1905 Henry Irving died, leaving the aging Stoker without a steady jot for the first time in his life. A year after Irving's death Stoker wrote "Personal Reminiscences of Henry Irving." Stoker managed to write other novels after this point until the time of his death in 1912 at the age of 64.

CHARLES DICKENS

This greatest of Victorian writers was born in Landport, Portsmouth, on February 7, 1812. His father John worked as a clerk in the Navy Payroll Office in Portsmouth. The elder Dickens was transfered several times, first to London, then to Chatham, and finally, in 1822, back to London, where the family lived in Camden Town.

John Dickens was constantly in debt, and in 1824 he was imprisoned in Marshalsea debtor's prison (Southwark). Charles was forced to leave school at the age of 12 and go to work in a bootblack factory to help support the Dickens family.

It was his personal experience of factory work and the living conditions of the poor that created in Dickens the compassion which was to mark his literary works such as *Oliver Twist.*

Dickens was released from the purgatory of Warren's Blacking Factory when his father received a legacy from a relative, and could finally pay his debts and be set free from Marshalsea. Charles went to Wellington House Academy for two years, then took work at Gray's Inn as a clerk.

Dickens worked as a Parliamentary reporter before finally moving on to *The Morning Chronicle* in 1834. His first published work appeared in *Monthly Magazine* in December 1833, and he followed it with nine more, penning his name as "Boz" to the last two articles. The pseudonym "Boz" was drawn from a pet name for his younger brother when they were children. In 1836 his articles were compiled and published as "*Sketches by Boz*".

Shortly after *Boz* was published, Dickens married, to Catherine Hogarth, the daughter of a co-worker at the Morning Chronicle newspaper. Together they had 10 children before they separated in 1858, but it was not Catherine but her younger sister, Mary, who was to prove the inspiration for many of Dicken's literary heroines. She remained to him an ideal of womanhood that found expression in his characters such as Rose Maylie (Oliver Twist), and Agnes Wickfield (David Copperfield).

Dickens followed up "*Sketches*" with his first commercial success, "*Pickwick Papers*" (more properly *The Posthumous Papers of the Pickwick Club*). This collection of 20 short stories was appeared in monthly installments and it became a publishing phenomenon - easily the most widely read literary work in English to that date.

Although the series was largely humorous, it also dealt with the grim social iniquities of the time, and it was this awareness and concern for the plight of the lower classes that was to mark much of Dickens' life work.

Dickens was working on another serialised novel while *Pickwick Papers* was running. This work proved to be one of his most enduring, a tale of innocence amid the squalor of London's criminal classes, *Oliver Twist*, which was published from 1837-38.

Dickens kept up his prodigious output, and *Nicholas Nickleby* followed quickly on the heels of *Oliver Twist*. In his new work Dickens tried to combine the humour of Pickwick with the cry for social reforms of Oliver. It worked, and sales of *Nicholas Nickleby* reached 50,000 copies evey month.

Dickens started his own magazine, a weekly titled *Master Humphrey's Clock*. In MHC he introduced the tragic heroine, Little Nell, in the serialised tale of *The Old Curiosity Shop*. It was this work which gave him international fame, and the name of Charles Dickens spread to the USA, where he was enormously popular.

In December 1843 Dickens wrote one of his most enduring works, the short story entitled *A Christmas Carol*. Lesser known Christmas tales followed in subsequent years, such as *The Chimes* (1844) and *The Cricket and the Hearth* (1845). In these stories and his longer works Dickens constantly returned to themes of social inequality and oppression of the poor.

The largely autobiographical *David Copperfield* followed in 1850. In that year he also helped found the Guild of Literature and Arts to assist struggling artists. The Guild raised money through public theatrical performances, and

Dickens was a regular performer at Guild events. He loved the stage, and it was this love of dramatic performance which he brought to public readings of his works.

Dickens literary output remained prolific, with later works including *A Tale of Two Cities* (1859), *Great Expectations* (1860-61), and Our Mutual Friend (1864-5). Charles Dickens died on June 9, 1870 and was buried at Westminster Abbey.

CHETAN BHAGAT

Chetan Bhagat (born 22 April 1974) is an Indian author, columnist and YouTuber. He was listed in Time magazine's list of World's 100 Most Influential People in 2010. Five of his novels have been adapted into films.

Bhagat grew up in a traditional Punjabi Hindu family. His father served as a lieutenant colonel in the Indian Army and his mother worked as a scientist in Indian Agricultural Research Institute, New Delhi.

He was schooled at the Army Public School, Dhaula Kuan. He claims to have been an average student at 15. His love for writing began during his school years. He used to write articles for the literary magazine of his school and seeing his name printed on the magazine as a writer encouraged him to continue writing.

Bhagat graduated with a B.Tech. degree in Mechanical Engineering from the Indian Institute of Technology, Delhi in 1995.

Bhagat pursued a Master of Business Administration degree in marketing from the Indian Institute of Management, Ahmedabad (IIMA) and graduated in 1997. In June 2018, IIMA awarded him the "Young Alumni Achiever's Awards 2018" in the Art & Entertainment category.

After graduating with a masters of business administration degree in 1998, Bhagat was placed through his campus at Peregrine Investments Holdings in Canada. However, he lost this job within six months as the company closed its operations in 1998.

His next job was as an investment banker with Goldman Sachs at their Hong Kong office. Despite being unhappy with his boss, he stayed and kept him in mind when he characterized the villain in his second novel One Night @ the Call Center.

He spent most of his time at the Goldman Sachs office in writing, completing and revising drafts of his first novel, Five Point Someone. After two years, Rupa Publications accepted his manuscript and offered to publish it.

By 2006, he was vice-president of Strategic Investment Group, Deutsche Bank in Hong Kong. His second novel, One Night @ the Call Center, was published in 2005 and became a best-seller. In March 2008, Bhagat moved back to India with his wife and three-year-old twin sons. He joined as a director in Deutsche Bank's distressed-assets team in Kodak House, Mumbai. The same year his third novel, The 3 Mistakes of My Life, was published and sold seven lakh (700,000) copies in three months.

In 2009, he quit his banking career to write full-time.

Bhagat is also a popular motivational speaker and has spoken at more than 800 organizations in 1000 cities around the world.

Bhagat started writing his first novel "Five Point Someone" when he was working at Goldman Sachs in Hong Kong in the early 2000s. In an interview, he said he wrote about 15 drafts of the novel and also sent the final manuscripts to several publishers.

The manuscript was finally accepted by the publishing house Rupa Publications in Delhi and was published in 2004. The novel narrates the story of three IIT students who consider themselves to be below average students among other students there. The story was adopted by film director Rajkumar Hirani into a film named "3 Idiots" starring Aamir Khan, R. Madhavan, Sharman Joshi, and Kareena Kapoor. It became one of the most successful Bollywood movies of all time.

After the success of his first novel, he started working on his second book "One Night @ the Call Center" which was published in 2005. The novel was also a success.

In the first three days of its release, almost 50,000 copies were sold. It became India's fastest selling book of its time. The book was also adapted into a movie named "Hello"; Chetan and Atul Agnihotri wrote the script for the movie.

Bhagat decided to make writing a full-time career. His third novel, "The 3 Mistakes of My Life", published in 2008, also was a bestseller. The Bollywood movie "Kai Po Che" is based on this novel.

Bhagat's fourth novel "2 States", published in 2009 was inspired by his relationship with his wife. The novel is about how he fell in love with a South Indian girl and the troubles he faced in his love life. The book was adapted into a movie of the same name starring Arjun Kapoor and Alia Bhatt and became a success.

Bhagat's later novels, "Revolution 2020", "Half Girlfriend" and "One Indian Girl" also gained commercial success.

His novels, "The Girl in Room 105", published in 2018, "One Arranged Murder", published in 2020 and his latest novel "400 days", published in 2021 were bestsellers.

Bhagat is also a YouTuber. His YouTube channel provides motivational tips to young Indians.

He launched a podcast show Deeptalk with Chetan Bhagat where he invites accomplished guests for a conversation about how they made it big in life.

EDGAR ALLAN POE

Edgar Allan Poe was born in Boston, Massachusetts, to parents who were itinerant actors. His father David Poe Jr. died probably in 1810. Elizabeth Hopkins Poe died in 1811, leaving three children. Edgar was taken into the home of a Richmond merchant John Allan. The remaining children were cared for by others. Poe's brother William died young and sister Rosalie become later insane. At the age of five Poe could recite passages of English poetry. Later one of his teachers in Richmond said: "While the other boys wrote mere mechanical verses, Poe wrote genuine poetry; the boy was a born poet."

Poe was brought up partly in England (1815-20), where he attended Manor School at Stoke Newington. Later it become the setting for his story 'William Wilson'. Never legally adopted, Poe took Allan's name for his middle name. Poe attended the University of Virginia (1826-27), but was expelled for not paying his gambling debts.

This led to quarrel with Allan, who refused to pay the debts. Allan later disowned him. In 1826 Poe became engaged to Elmira Royster, but her parents broke off the engagement. During his stay at the university, Poe composed some tales, but little is known of his apprentice works.

In 1827 Poe joined the U.S. Army as a common soldier under assumed name, Edgar A. Perry. He was sent to Sullivan's Island, South Carolina, which provided settings for 'The Gold Bug' (1843) and 'The Balloon Hoax' (1844). *Tamerlane and Other Poems* (1827), which Poe published at his own expense, sold poorly. It has become one of the rarest volumes in American literary history. In 1830 Poe entered West Point. He was dishonorably discharged next year, for intentional neglect of his duties - apparently as a result of his own determination to be released.

In 1833 Poe lived in Baltimore with his father's sister Mrs. Maria Clemm. After winning a prize of $50 for the short story 'MS Found in a Bottle,' he started career as a staff member of various magazines, among others the *Southern Literary Messenger* in Richmond (1835-37), *Burton's Gentleman's Magazine* in Philadelphia (1839-40), and *Graham's Magazine* (1842-43).

During these years he wrote some of his best-known stories. *Southern Literary Messenger* he had to leave partly due to his alcoholism.

In 1836 Poe married his 13-year-old cousin Virginia Clemm. She bust a blood vessel in 1842, and remained a virtual invalid until her death from tuberculosis five years later. After the death of his wife, Poe began to lose his struggle with drinking and drugs. He had several romances, including an affair with the poet Sarah Helen Whitman, who said: "His proud reserve, his profound melancholy, his unworldliness - may we not say his *unearthliness* of nature - made his character one very difficult of comprehension to the casual observer." In 1849 Poe become again engaged to Elmira Royster, who was at that time Mrs. Shelton. To Virginia he addressed the famous poem 'Annabel Lee' (1849) - its subject, Poe's favorite, is the death of a beautiful woman.

For the moon never beams without bringing me dreams
Of the beautiful Annabel Lee;
And the stars never rise but I feel the bright eyes
Of the beautiful Annabel Lee;
And so, all the night-time, I lie down by the side
Of my darling - my darling - my life and my bride,
In the sepulchre there by the sea,
In her tomb by the sounding sea.
(from 'Annabel Lee', 1849)

Poe's first collection, *Tales of the Grotesque and Arabesque,* appeared in 1840. It contained one of his most famous work, 'The Fall of the House of Usher.' In the story the narrator visits the crumbling mansion of his friend, Roderick Usher, and tries to dispel Roderick's gloom.

Although his twin sister, Madeline, has been placed in the family vault dead, Roderick is convinced she lives. Madeline arises in trance, and carries her brother to death. The house itself splits asunder and sinks into the tarn. The tale has inspired several film adaptations.

Roger Corman's version from 1960, starring Mark Damon, Harry Ellerbe, Myrna Fahey, and Vincent Price, was the first of the director's Poe movies.

The Raven (1963) collected old stars of the horror genre, Vincent Price, Peter, Lorre, and Boris Karloff. According to the director, Price and Lorre "drove Boris a little crazy" - the actor was not used to improvised dialogue. Corman filmed the picture in fifteen days, using revamped portions of his previous Poe sets.

In *Narrative of Arthur Gordon Pym* (1838), Poe's longest tale, the secret theme is the terror of whiteness. Poe invented tribes that live near the Antarctic Circle. The strange bestial humans are black, even down to their teeth. They have been exposed to the terrible visitations of men and white storms.

These are mixed together, and they slaughter the crew of Pym's vessel. The Argentinean writer Jorge Luis Borges has assumed that Poe chose the color intuitively, or for the same reasons as in Melville explained in the chapter 'The Whiteness of the Whale' in his *Moby Dick*.

Later the 'lost world' idea was developed by Edgar Rice Burroughs in *The Land That Time Forgot* (1924) and other works.

During the early 1840s, Poe's best-selling work was curiously *The Conchologist's First Book* (1839). It was based on Thomas Wyatt's work, which sold poorly because of its high prize.

Wyatt was Poe's friend and asked him to abridge the book and put his own name on its title page - the publisher had strongly opposed any idea of producing a cheaper edition. *The Conchologist's First Book* was a success. Its first edition was sold out in two months and other editions followed.

The dark poem of lost love, 'The Raven,' brought Poe national fame, when it appeared in 1845. "With me poetry has been not a purpose, but a passion; and the passions should be held in reverence: they must not - they cannot at will be excited, with an eye to the paltry compensations, or the more paltry commendations, of mankind." (from *The Raven and Other Poems*, preface, 1845)

In a lecture in Boston the author said that the two most effective letters in the English language were *o* and *r* - this inspired the expression "nevermore" in '*The Raven*', and because a parrot is unworthy of the dignity of poetry, a raven could well repeat the word at the end of each stanza.

Lenore rhymed with "nevermore." The poems has inspired a number of artists. Perhaps the most renowed are Gustave Doré's (1832-1883) melancholic illustrations.

Poe suffered from bouts of depression and madness, and he attempted suicide in 1848. In September the following year he disappeared for three days after a drink at a birthday party and on his way to visit his new fiancée in Richmond. He turned up in delirious condition in Baltimore gutter and died on October 7, 1849.

Poe's work and his theory of "pure poetry" was early recognized especially in France, where he inspired Jules Verne, Charles Baudelaire (1821-1867), Paul Valéry (1871-1945) and Stéphane Mallarmé (1842-1898). "In Edgar Poe," wrote Baudelaire, "there is no tiresome snivelling; but everywhere and at all times an indefatigable enthusiasm in seeking the ideal." In America Emerson called him "the jingle man." Poe's influence is seen in many other modern writers, as in Junichiro Tanizaki's early stories and Kobo Abe's novels, or more clearly in the development of the19th century detective novel. J.L. Borges, R.L. Stevenson, and a vast general readership, have been impressed by the stories which feature Poe's detective Dupin ('The Murders in the Rue Morgue', 1841; 'The Purloined Letter,' 1845) and the morbid metaphysical speculation of 'The Facts in the Case of M. Waldermar' (1845).

Thomas M. Disch has argued in his *The Dreams Our Stuff Is Made Of* (1998) that it was actually Poe who was the originator of the modern science fiction. One of his tales, 'Mellonta Taunta' (1840) describes a future society, an anti-Utopia, in which Poe satirizes his own times. Another tales in this vein are 'The Thousand-and-Second Tale of Sceherazade' and 'A Descent into the Maelstrom'.

However, Poe was not concerned with any specific scientific concept but mostly explored different realities, one of the central concerns of science fiction ever since.

In his supernatural fiction Poe usually dealt with paranoia rooted in personal psychology, physical or mental enfeeblement, obsessions, the damnation of death, feverish fantasies, the cosmos as source of horror and inspiration, without bothering himself with such supernatural beings as ghosts, werewolves, vampires, and so on.

Some of his short stories are humorous, among them 'The Devil in the Belfry,' 'The Duc de l'Omelette,' 'Bon-Bon' and 'Never Bet the Devil Your Head,' all of which employ the Devil as an ironic figure of fun. - Poe was also one of the most prolific literary journalists in American history, one whose extensive body of reviews and criticism has yet to be collected fully. James Russell Lowell (1819-91) once wrote about Poe: "Three fifths of him genius and two fifths sheer fudge."

ERNEST HEMINGWAY

Ernest Hemingway was born on July 21, 1899, in Oak Park, Illinois, an affluent suburb just west of Chicago, to Clarence Edmonds Hemingway, a physician, and Grace Hall Hemingway, a musician.

Ernest Hemingway, widely regarded as one of the greatest American writers of the 20th century, left an indelible mark on the world of literature. His concise and powerful writing style, coupled with his adventurous lifestyle, made him an enduring literary icon. From his early days as a journalist to his Pulitzer Prize-winning novels, this biography delves into the life and legacy of Ernest Hemingway.

Ernest Miller Hemingway was the second of six children born to Clarence and Grace Hemingway. His father was a physician, and his mother was a devout Christian. The Hemingway family valued education, and young Ernest spent much of his childhood engrossed in books. He developed a love for the outdoors and enjoyed fishing and hunting in the pristine wilderness of northern Michigan.

Hemingway's early experiences would profoundly shape his writing. His exposure to nature, his father's passion for science, and his mother's religious upbringing created a complex tapestry of influences that would surface in his works. At Oak Park and River Forest High School, Hemingway excelled in English classes and participated in various sports, including boxing and football.

After graduating from high school in 1917, Hemingway briefly worked as a reporter for the Kansas City Star. The newspaper's style guide, emphasizing succinct and direct writing, left a lasting impact on his prose. In 1918, he volunteered for service in World War I and joined the American Red Cross as an ambulance driver in Italy. His experiences on the Italian frontlines, witnessing the horrors of war, would profoundly influence his future writing.

During the war, Hemingway was wounded by mortar fire and spent several months in a hospital in Milan. Upon his return to the United States, he met and married Hadley Richardson, beginning a tumultuous personal life that would leave its mark on his writing.

In the 1920s, Hemingway moved to Paris with Hadley, where he became part of a vibrant community of expatriate writers and artists. This period, often referred to as the "Lost

Generation," included Gertrude Stein, F. Scott Fitzgerald, and Ezra Pound, among others. Hemingway's experiences in Paris allowed him to develop his craft and refine his distinctive writing style.

During this time, Hemingway published his first major work, "The Sun Also Rises" (1926), a novel that captured the disillusionment and aimlessness felt by many in the aftermath of World War I. The book's spare prose and honest portrayal of post-war life established Hemingway as a leading voice in American literature.

Ernest Hemingway's writing style was characterized by brevity, simplicity, and a focus on themes such as masculinity, war, and human endurance.

He believed in the power of understatement, favoring concise sentences that conveyed strong emotions and vivid imagery. His sparse yet evocative prose resonated with readers, making him one of the most influential writers of his time.

In addition to "The Sun Also Rises," Hemingway produced several other notable works. "A Farewell to Arms" (1929) drew on his experiences as an ambulance driver and explored the futility of war and the fragility of love. "For Whom the Bell Tolls" (1940) depicted the Spanish Civil War and highlighted the heroism and sacrifice of its characters. Both novels became celebrated classics.

Hemingway's fascination with adventure and his love of hunting and fishing found expression in "The Old Man and the Sea" (1952), a novella that won him the Pulitzer Prize for Fiction. The story of an aging fisherman's struggle against nature showcased Hemingway's ability to convey profound themes through simple yet powerful storytelling.

Hemingway's personal life was marked by a series of turbulent relationships and restless travels. He divorced Hadley in 1927 and married three more times. He lived in various locations, including Key West, Cuba, and Spain, where he actively participated in bullfighting and big-game hunting.

In the 1930s, Hemingway reported on the Spanish Civil War, which fueled his passion for political activism. He supported the Republican cause against General Francisco Franco's forces and wrote articles criticizing fascism. However, the war's brutality and the rise of totalitarian regimes deeply affected him.

As Hemingway grew older, he faced declining mental and physical health. He suffered from bouts of depression and alcoholism, and his writing output decreased. Tragedy struck on July 2, 1961, when Hemingway took his own life with a shotgun at his home in Ketchum, Idaho. He left behind a legacy of exceptional literature and a complex, enigmatic persona.

Ernest Hemingway's impact on American literature is immeasurable. His unique writing style, characterized by economy of language and emotional depth, influenced generations of writers. Hemingway's themes of masculinity, war, and the human experience continue to resonate with readers today.

His books have become literary classics, studied in schools and universities around the world. Hemingway's influence can be seen in the works of authors such as Cormac McCarthy and Raymond Carver, who adopted his minimalist writing style. The "Hemingwayesque" approach to storytelling remains an enduring hallmark of modern American literature.

In recognition of his contributions to literature, Hemingway was awarded the Nobel Prize in Literature in 1954. His name is synonymous with literary excellence and the pursuit of authenticity in both life and art.

Ernest Hemingway's life was as vibrant and adventurous as his writing. From his early experiences as a journalist and ambulance driver in World War I to his time in Paris and his later travels, Hemingway constantly sought inspiration and new challenges. Through his concise and powerful prose, he captured the essence of the human condition and left an indelible mark on the literary world.

While Hemingway's personal life was marked by tumultuous relationships and battles with mental health, his legacy endures. His works continue to captivate readers, and his writing style remains an influential force in modern literature. As we reflect on his life and literary achievements, we honor the legacy of Ernest Hemingway, a true literary icon.

GEORGE BERNARD SHAW

George Bernard Shaw was born in Dublin, the son of a civil servant. His education was irregular, due to his dislike of any organized training. After working in an estate agent's office for a while he moved to London as a young man (1876), where he established himself as a leading music and theatre critic in the eighties and nineties and became a prominent member of the Fabian Society, for which he composed many pamphlets.

He began his literary career as a novelist; as a fervent advocate of the new theatre of Ibsen (*The Quintessence of Ibsenism*, 1891) he decided to write plays in order to illustrate his criticism of the English stage. His earliest dramas were called appropriately *Plays Pleasant and Unpleasant* (1898). Among these, *Widower's Houses* and *Mrs. Warren's Profession* savagely attack social hypocrisy, while in plays such as *Arms and the Man* and *The Man of Destiny* the criticism is less fierce.

Shaw's radical rationalism, his utter disregard of conventions, his keen dialectic interest and verbal wit often turn the stage into a forum of ideas, and nowhere more openly than in the famous discourses on the Life Force, «Don Juan in Hell», the third act of the dramatization of woman's love chase of man, *Man and Superman* (1903).

In the plays of his later period discussion sometimes drowns the drama, in *Back to Methuselah* (1921), although in the same period he worked on his masterpiece *Saint Joan* (1923), in which he rewrites the well-known story of the French maiden and extends it from the Middle Ages to the present.

Other important plays by Shaw are *Caesar and Cleopatra* (1901), a historical play filled with allusions to modern times, and *Androcles and the Lion* (1912), in which he exercised a kind of retrospective history and from modern movements drew deductions for the Christian era.

In *Major Barbara* (1905), one of Shaw's most successful «discussion» plays, the audience's attention is held by the power of the witty argumentation that man can achieve aesthetic salvation only through political activity, not as an individual.

The Doctor's Dilemma (1906), facetiously classified as a tragedy by Shaw, is really a comedy the humour of which is directed at the medical profession.

Candida (1898), with social attitudes toward sex relations as objects of his satire, and *Pygmalion* (1912), a witty study of phonetics as well as a clever treatment of middle-class morality and class distinction, proved some of Shaw's greatest successes on the stage. It is a combination of the dramatic, the comic, and the social corrective that gives Shaw's comedies their special flavour.

He was awarded the Nobel Prize for Literature in 1925. Shaw's complete works appeared in thirty-six volumes between 1930 and 1950, the year of his death.

GUY DE MAUPASSANT

Guy de Maupassant was probably born at the Château de Miromesniel, Dieppe. His paternal ancestors were noble, and his maternal grandfather, Paul Le Poittevin, was Gustave Flaubert's godfather. His parents separated when he was 11 years old. Maupassant grew up in his native Normandy. The gift of a photographic memory enabled him to gather a storehouse of information, which later helped him in his stories about the Norman people.

In his teens Maupassant was shown, by the poet Algernon Swinburne (1837-1909), a mummified hand. He used this haunting image in his early short story 'La Main Ecorchée (1875). In 1869 Maupassant started to study law in Paris, but soon, at age 20, he volunteered to serve in the army during Franco-Prussian War. After his return to Paris, Maupassant joined the literary circle of Gustave Flaubert. He was a friend of Maupassant's mother's friend, and introduced him to some of the leading writers, among them Émile Zola, Ivan Turgenev, and Henry James. From Flaubert, who was obsessed with the writer's craft, Maupassant learned the exactness and accuracy of observations, and balance and precision of style.

Between the years 1872 and 1880 Maupassant was a civil servant, first at the ministry of maritime affairs, then at the ministry of education. As a poet Maupassant made his debut with *Des Vers* (1880). In the same year he published in the anthology *Soirées de Medan* (1880), edited by E. Zola, his masterpiece, *Boule de Suif* (Ball of Fat, 1880). The story is set during the Franco-Prussian War.

A well-known prostitute, nicknamed 'Boule de Suif', is traveling in a coach with bourgeois fellow passengers. They are detained by a Prussian officer who will not allow the coach to proceed until Boule de Suif gives her to him, which she refuses on principle to do: *"Kindly tell that scoundrel, that cur, that carrion of a Prussian, that I will never consent—you understand?—never, never, never!"* However, the other passagers start to get bored and press her to yield to the officers demands.

After swallowing her pride she spends a night with him and in the morning she is treated by the group as if she had been infected with some deadly disease. *"No one looked at her, no one thought of her. She felt herself swallowed up in the scorn of these virtuous creatures, who had first sacrificed, then rejected her as a thing useless and unclean. Then she remembered her big basket full of the good things they had so greedily devoured: the two chickens coated in jelly, the pies, the pears, the four bottles of claret; and her fury broke forth like a cord that is overstrained, and she was on the verge of tears. She made terrible efforts at self-control, drew herself up, swallowed the sobs which choked her; but the tears rose nevertheless, shone at the brink of her eyelids, and soon two heavy drops coursed slowly down her cheeks."*

It has often been said that the American director John Ford borrowed the plot to his film *Stagecoach* (1939). Ford knew the story, but Ernest Haycox's character study 'Stage to Lordsburg' served for the director as the framework for his famous morality play. Partly for commercial reasons the *Stagecoach* team hide their 'arty' source. In the film a group of people travel by stage to Lordsburg, passing through Indian territory. The socially respected passengers turn out to be hypocrites, thieves, and unworthy characters, whereas the outsiders win their faults or show bravery and compassion. Claire Trevor played the good-hearted prostitute Dallas and John Wayne in the role of the Ringo Kidd was catapulted to stardom.

During the 1880s Maupassant created some 300 short stories, six novels, three travel books, and one volume of verse. In tone, his tales were marked by objectivity, highly controlled style, and sometimes sheer comedy. Usually they were built around simple episodes from everyday life, which revealed the hidden sides of people. On several occasions were narrated in the first person or were tales told by a named character. In 'The Jewels of M. Lantin' the chief clerk of the Minister of the Interior, marries the daughter of a provincial tax collector. He is unbelievably happy. She has only two small vices - her love of the theater and her passion for artificial jewels. One wintry evening she comes from the opera shivering with cold and a week later she dies

Lantin is haunted by his memories, and plunges into poverty. He takes her necklace to a jeweler who tells that it is very valuable. Lantin has believed that his wife's jewelry were fakes because she could not have purchased valuable items. He realizes that they were gifts and the truth makes him weep bitterly. *"As he walked along, Lantin said to himself, "How easy it is to be happy when you're rich! With money you can even shake off your sorrows; you can go or stay as you please! You can travel and amuse yourself."* He sells her jewelry, resigns from his work, and enjoys the theater for the first time in his life. *"Six months later he married. His second wife was a most worthy woman, but rather difficult. She made his life unbearable."*

Among Maupassant's best know books is *Une Vie* (A Woman's Life, 1883), about the frustrating existence of a Norman wife, *Bel-Ami* (1885), which depicts an unscrupulous journalist. *Pierre et Jean* (1888) was a psychological study of two brothers. The novel was thought to be immoral because the hero succeeds by doing wrong. Maupassant's most upsetting horror story, *Le Horla* (1887), was about madness and suicide.

The nameless protagonist is perhaps a syphilitic. In the beginning of the story the narrator - a prosperous young Norman gentleman - sees a Brazilian three-master boat flow by his house. He salutes it and the gesture evidently summons the Horla, an invisible being. The Horlas are cousins of the vampires and their advent means that the reign of man is over. Our narrator eventually sets fire to his own house, to destroy his Horla, but his servants die in the fire. He realizes that his Horla is still alive and decides to kill himself.

Maupassant had suffered from his 20s from syphilis. The disease later caused increasing mental disorder - also seen in his nightmarish stories, which have much in common with Edgar Allan Poe's supernatural visions. Critics have charted

Maupassant's developing illness through his semi-autobiographical stories of abnormal psychology, but the theme of mental disorder is present in his first collection, *La Maison Tellier* (1881), published at the height of his health.

Maupassant's horror fiction consists of some 39 stories, only a tenth of his total. Recurring theme in these is madness: 'A Night in Paris' is a paranoid nightmare: its narrator feels compelled to walk the streets, in 'Who Knows?' the narrator sufferers from delusions about the furniture of his house, 'A Madman' is a story about a judge, who commits murder, just for the experience, and condemns an innocent man to death for the crime.

'The Inn' has much similarities with Stephen King's famous novel *The Shining*. Maupassant describes two caretakers, living in the French Alps in an remote inn, which is surrounded by snow six months and unreachable. When the older caretaker goes missing, the younger in his loneliness loses his reason. 'The Hand', about a severed human hand which, despite chained up, escapes and strangles its owner, has inspired several writers and movie directors (1946, dir. by Robert Florey; 1960, dir. by Henry Cass; 1981, dir. by Oliver Stone, from the novel *The Lizard's Tail*).

On January 2, in 1892, Maupassant tried to commit suicide by cutting his throat and was committed to the celebrated private asylum of Dr. Esprit Blanche at Passy, in Paris, where he died next year. It is claimed that all his fiction came from his own experience. Although he probably fictionalized true occurrences or tales told to him, Maupassant's style has been imitated by countless writers and his influence can be seen on such masters of the short story as W. Somerset Maugham and O. Henry.

HERMAN MELVILLE

Herman Melville (1819-1891). Herman Melville's life is a mystery. No one has satisfactorily explained, although many have tried, why the 32-year-old author of the monumental novel Moby Dick would for the next 40 years write nothing of consequence. And no one can understand why a hardy seafarer like Melville, who had experienced the delights and hardships of the South Seas both aboard ship and on shore, should spend most of his last 19 years at the humdrum job of customs inspector. Perhaps the answer lies in Melville's early background. Descended from old American stock, Herman Melville was born in New York, the son of a prosperous dry goods importer whose business later failed.

Melville's father died when Herman was only 13, and he left his family in a dire financial state. Melville was forced to make his way in the world at an early age. He was mortified at his family's loss of stature, and the remainder of his life seemed to involve a quest for security and inner peace.

After halfhearted attempts at being a bank clerk, a teacher, and a cabin boy, Melville finally shipped out to sea on a whaler bound for the South Seas. For the 1st time the world opened up to him. The beauty and the cruelty of the sea caught him forever in its spell. When his ship reached the Marquesas Islands (now part of French Polynesia), Melville and a companion jumped ship and lived among the pleasure-loving (and cannibalistic) natives. But despite his attachment to an island girl, Melville became homesick and signed on a passing whaler. This voyage did not last long, for he joined a mutiny and landed in a Tahitian jail—from which he promptly escaped.

Melville renewed his wanderings among the islanders and rapidly stored up the knowledge that was to serve him so well in his books. But he still yearned for home and therefore joined the crew of another whaler as a harpooner. He left this ship in Hawaii and shortly thereafter began the last leg of his journey home by joining the crew of a U.S. naval frigate as an able-bodied seaman. When Melville arrived back in America he had everything he needed to inspire 6 years of magnificent creativity as a novelist.

In 1846, Typee appeared, the 1st of 2 novels based on Melville's South Seas experiences. A mixture of fact and highly colored fiction, it was greeted with enthusiasm and outrage. Missionaries were particularly offended by the negative view it presented of their activities, and in later editions Melville was forced to make deletions to soothe their injured feelings. Omoo followed the next year and established the author's literary reputation, which was further enhanced by the publication of White Jacket. This latter novel fully exposed the cruelty then extant in the U.S. Navy and was the direct cause of the elimination of flogging as a punishment.

All this artistic effort culminated in the stunning Moby Dick. Melville began this book as a mere retelling of old sailors' yarns about a huge albino whale named Mocha Dick or Moby Dick, but in the process he transformed it into a novel so magnificent that it defies both description and critical analysis.

After Pierre appeared in 1852, Melville's creative energy rapidly dried up. He was now either afraid of or tired of writing. Some poetry, a satire, and a handful of short stories were all that were left in him. His popularity dwindled until he had to publish his last works at his own expense.

His brilliant short novel Billy Budd was not published until 33 years after his death. Financial problems pressed in upon him and domestic tragedy marred his life. One son killed himself either accidentally or deliberately, and another ran away from home. Melville repeatedly sought government employment and was greatly relieved when, in 1866, he was appointed a customs inspector in New York City, a job that he held for 19 years. When he died, only one newspaper bothered to publish an obituary. Many years passed before his true greatness was recognized.

H.G. WELLS

Herbert George Wells was born in Bromley, Kent. His father was a shopkeeper and a professional cricketer until he broke his leg. In his early childhood Wells developed love for literature. His mother served from time to time as a housekeeper at the nearby estate of Uppark, and young Wells studied books in the library secretly. When his father's business failed, Wells was apprenticed like his brothers to a draper. He spent the years between 1880 and 1883 in Windsor and Southsea, and later recorded them in *Kipps* (1905). In the story Arthur Kipps is raised by his aunt and uncle. Kipps is also apprenticed to a draper. After learning that he has been left a fortune, Kipps enters the upper-class society, which Wells describes with sharp social criticism.

In 1883 Wells became a teacher/pupil at Midhurst Grammar School. He obtained a scholarship to the Normal School of Science in London and studied there biology under T.H. Huxley. However, his interest faltered and in 1887 he left without a degree. He taught in private schools for four years, not taking his B.S. degree until 1890. Next year he settled in London, married his cousin Isabel and continued his career as a teacher in a correspondence college. From 1893 Wells became a full-time writer.

Wells left Isabel for one of his brightest students, Amy Catherine, whom he married in 1895. As a novelist Wells made his debut with *The Time Machine*, a parody of English class division. The narrator is Hillyer, who discusses with his friends about theories of time travel. A week later their host has an incredible story to tell - he has returned from the year 802701. The Time Traveler had found two people: the Eloi, weak and little, who live above ground in a seemingly Edenic paradise, and the Morlocks, bestial creatures that live below ground, who eat the Eloi. The Traveler's beautiful friend Weena is killed, he flees into the far future, where he encounters "crab-like creatures" and things "like a huge white butterfly", that have taken over the planet.

In the year 30,000,000 he finds lichens, blood-red sea and a creature with tentacles. He returns horrified back to the present. Much of the realistic atmosphere of the story was achieved by carefully studied technical details. The basic principles of the machine contained materials regarding time as the fourth dimension - years later Albert Einstein published his theory of the four dimensional continuum of space-time.

The Time Machine was followed by THE ISLAND OF DR. MOREAU (1896), in which a mad scientist transforms animals into human creatures. The story is told in flashback by a man named Prendick. He travels with a biologist to a remote island, which is controlled by Dr. Moreau. In his laboratory he experiments with animals, and has created Beast People. Moreau is killed by Puma-Woman. Prendick escapes from the island, and returns to London. He concludes the tale: *"Even then it seemed that I, too, was not a reasonable creature, but only an animal tormented with some strange disorder in its brain, that sent it to wander alone, like as sheep stricken with the gid."* Wells, who was a Darwinist, did not reject the evolutionary theory but attacked optimists and warned that human progress is not inevitable. In film versions the character of Dr. Moreau has inspired such actors as Charles Laughton, Burt Lancaster, and Marlon Brando.

The Invisible Man (1897) was a Faustian story of a scientist who has tampered with nature in pursuit of superhuman powers, and *The War of the Worlds* (1898), a novel of an invasion of Martians. The story appeared at a time when Schiaparell's discovery of Martian "canals" Percival Lowell's book *Mars* (1895) arose speculations that there could be life on the Red Planet. The narrator is an unnamed "philosophical writer" who tells about events that happened six years earlier. Martian cylinders land on earth outside London and the invaders, who have a "roundish bulk with tentacles" start to vaporize humans. The Martians build walking tripods which ruin towns.

Panic spreads, London is evacuated. Martians release poisonous black smoke. However, Martians are slain "by the humblest things that God, in his wisdom, has put on this earth." In 1930 Paramount offered the story to the Soviet director Sergei Eisenstein, but he never attempted an adaptation. Its later Hollywood version from 1953 reflected

Cold War attitudes. *The First Men on the Moon* (1901) was prophetic description of the methodology of space flight, and *The War in the Air* (1908) foresaw the importance of air forces in combat. Although Wells's novels were highly entertaining, he also tried to arise debate about the future of mankind.

Dissatisfied with his literary work, Wells moved into the novel genre with *Love and Mr. Lewisham* (1900). Kipps strengthened his reputation as a serous writer. Wells also published critical pamphlets attacking the Victorian social order, among them *Anticipations* (1901), *Mankind in the Making* (1903), and *A Modern Utopia* (1905). In *The History of Mr. Polly* (1909) Wells returned to vanished England.

Passionate concern for society led Wells to join in 1903 the socialist Fabian Society in London. It advocated a fairer society by planning for a gradual system of reforms. However, he soon quarreled with the society's leaders, among them George Bernard Shaw. This experience was basis for his novel *The New Machiavelli* (1911), which portrayed the noted Fabians.

At the outbreak of war in 1914, Wells was involved in a love affair with a young journalist, Rebecca West, 26 years his junior. West and Wells called themselves "panther" and "jaguar". Their son Anthony West later wrote about their difficult relationship in *Aspects of a Life* (1984).

In his novels Wells used his two wives, Amber Reeves, Rebecca West, Odette Keun and all the passing mistresses as models for his characters. "I was never a great amorist," Wells wrote in *Experiment in Autobiography* (1934) "though I have loved several people very deeply." Rebecca West became a famous author and married a wealthy banker, Henry

Andrews, who had business interests in Germany. Elizabeth von Arnim dismissed Wells, and Moura Budberg, Maxim Gorky's former mistress, refused to marry him or even be faithful.

"Nothing could have been more obvious to the people of the early twentieth century than the rapidity with which war was becoming impossible. And as certainly they did not see it. They did not see it until the atomic bombs burst in their fumbling hands." (from The World Set Free, 1914)

After WW I Wells published several non-fiction works, among them *The Outline of History* (1920), *The Science of Life* (1929-39), written in collaboration with Sir Julian Huxley and George Philip Wells, and *Experiment in Autobiography* (1934). At this time Wells had gained the status as a popular celebrity, and he continued to write prolifically. In 1917 he was a member of Research Committee for the League of Nations and published several books about the world organization.

Although Wells had many reservations about the Soviet system, he understood the broad aims of the Russian Revolution, and had in 1920 a fairly amiable meeting with Lenin. In the early 1920s Wells was a labour candidate for Parliament. Between the years 1924 and 1933 Wells lived mainly in France. From 1934 to 1946 he was the International president of PEN.

In 1934 he had discussions with both Stalin, who left him disillusioned, and Roosevelt, trying to recruit them without success to his world-saving schemes. Wells was convinced that Western socialists cannot compromise with Communism, and that the best hope for the future lay in Washington. Also one of his mistresses, Moura Budberg, turned out to be a Soviet agent for years. In *The Holy Terror* (1939) Wells studied the psychological development of a modern dictator exemplified in the careers of Stalin, Mussolini, and Hitler.

"The professional military mind is by necessity an inferior and unimaginative mind; no man of high intellectual quality would willingly imprison his gifts in such calling." (from The Outline of History, *1920)*

Orson Welles' Mercury Theater radio broadcast, based on *The War of the Worlds*, caused a panic in the Eastern United States on October 30, 1938.

In Newark, New Jersey, all the occupants of a block of flats left their homes with wet towels round their heads and in Harlem a congregation fell to its knees. Welles, who first considered the show silly, was shaken by the panic he had unleashed and promised that he would never do anything like it again. Later Welles attempted to claim authorship for the script, but it was written by Howard Koch, whose inside story of the whole episode, *The panic broadcast; portrait of an event*, appeared in 1970.

Wells himself was not amused with the radio play. He met the young director in 1940 at a San Antonio radio station, but was at that time mellowed and advertised Welles next film, *Citizen Kane*.

"Those who have not read The War of the Worlds *may be surprised to find that, like much of Wells's writing, it is full of poetry and contains passages that catch the throat. Wells tried to pretend that he was not an artist and stated that "there will come a time for every work of art when it will have served its purpose and be bereft of its last rag of significance." This has not yet happened for the best of Wells's science fiction, though it has done so for all but a few of his*

realistic and political novels." (Arthur C. Clarke in Greetings, Carbon-Based Bipeds!, 1999)

Wells lived through World War II in his house on Regent's Park, refusing to let the blitz drive him out of London. His last book, *Mind at the End of Its Tether* (1945), expressed pessimism about mankind's future prospects. Wells died in London on August 13. 1946. *"Human history becomes more and more a race between education and catastrophe." (from The Outline of History*, 1920)

H. H. MUNRO

Saki was born Hector Hugh Munro in Akyab, Burma (now Myanmar), the son of Charles Augustus Munro, an inspector-general in the Burma police. Munro's mother, the former Mary Frances Mercer, died in 1872 - she was killed by a runaway cow in an English country lane. Munro was brought up in England with his brother and sister by aunts who frequently used the birch and whip.

He was educated at Pencarwick School in Exmouth and Bedford Grammar School. From 1887 he traveled with his family in France, Germany and Switzerland. In 1891 his father settled in Devon, where he worked as a teacher. In 1893

Munro joined the Burma police. Three years later he was back in England and started his career as a journalist, writing for the *Westminster Gazette*.

In 1900 Munro's first book, *The Rise of the Russian Empire*, appeared. It is a historical study modelled upon Gibbon's famous *The Decline and Fall of the Roman Empire*. The book was received with hostile reviews in America.

It was followed in 1902 with a collection of short stories, *Not-so-Stories*. From 1902 to 1908 Munro worked as a foreign correspondent for *The Morning Post* in the Balkans, Russia and Paris, and then returned to London. In 1914 his novel *When William Came* appeared, in which he portrayed what might happen if the German emperor conquered England.´

"Only the old and the clergy of Established churches know how to be flippant gracefully," commented Reginald; "which reminds me that in the Anglican Church in a certain foreign capital, which shall be nameless, I was present the other day when one of the junior chaplains was preaching in aid of distressed somethings or other, and he brought a really eloquent passage to a close with the remark, 'The tears of the afflicted, to what shall I liken them—to diamonds?'

The other junior chaplain, who had been dozing out of professional jealousy, awoke with a start and asked hurriedly, 'Shall I play to diamonds, partner?' (from Reginald in Russia, 1910)

After the outbreak of World War I, although officially too old, Munro volunteered for the army as an ordinary soldier. He was killed by a sniper's bullet on November 14, 1916 in France, near Beaumont-Hamel. Munro was sheltering in a shell crater.

His last words, according to several sources, were: "Put that damned cigarette out!" After his death, his sister Ethel destroyed most of his papers and wrote her own account of their childhood. Like her brother, Ethel never married.

Saki's best fables are often more macabre than Kipling's. In his early stories Saki often portrayed eccentric characters, familiar from Oscar Wilde's plays. Among Saki's most frequently anthologized short stories is 'Tobermory', in which a cat, who has seen too much scandal through country house windows, learns to talk and starts to repeat the guests' vicious comments about each other.

'The Open Window' was a tale-within-a-tale. In the short story 'Sredni Vashtar' from *The Chronicles of Clovis* (1911) a young boy makes an idol of his illicit pet ferret. It kills his oppressive cousin and guardian, Mrs. De Ropp, modelled on Saki's aunt Agnes. "Sredni Vashtar went forth, *His thoughts were red thoughts and his teeth / were white. / His enemies called to peace, but he brought / them death*. Sredni Vashtar the Beautiful."

Saki was a misogynist, anti-Semite, and reactionary, who also did not take himself too serious. His stories, "true enough to be interesting and not true enough to be tiresome", were considered ideal reading for schoolboys.

However, Saki did not have any interest in safeguarding the Edwardian way of life. "Saki writes like an enemy, " said V.S. Pritchett later. "Society has bored him to the point of murder. Out laughter is only a note or two short of a scream of fear." In 'Laura' the title character is first reincarnated as a destructive otter after her death, and then as a naked brown Nubian boy.

Reginald and Clovis, two of his most famous heroes, appeared in a series of stories in which the two soul mates of Wilhelm Busch's Max and Moritz shock the conventional world or leave the reader to read between the lines.

When Amabel asks Reginald's help to supervise "the annual outing of the bucolic infants who composed the local choir", Reginald's eyes start to shine "with the dangerous enthusiasm of a convert." Once Reginald states: "People may say what they like about the decay of Christianity; the religious system that produced green Chartreuse can never really die."

J.K. ROWLING

J.K. Rowling was born on July 31, 1965, Chipping Sodbury, near Bristol, England. British author, creator of the popular and critically acclaimed Harry Potter series about a young sorcerer in training. Her given name at birth was Joanne Kathleen. Ms. Rowling has one sister, Di, who was born 2 years after J K.

It is interesting to note that Ms. Rowling claims that she has actually been writing since she was 5 or 6 years old. Her first story, called Rabbit, was filled with interesting characters, such as a large bee called Miss Bee.

Ms. Rowling, along with her parents and sister, moved twice while J K was growing up. While at one of their homes, close to Bristol and in Winterbourne, she had friends next door whose last name was Potter. J K never forgot the children, or the last name, which she liked very much.

When she was nine years old her family moved again to Tutshill. Ms. Rowling attended a primary (grade) school in Tutshill, and later attended Wyedean Comprehensive.

Ms. Rowling describes herself as being shy, freckly, with no natural athletic ability but a great love of literature. Later, when she graduated from Wyedean Comprehensive, she attended Exeter University.

Here Ms. Rowling studied French after her parents encouraged her into what they believed would be a wonderful career as a bilingual secretary. After graduation, however, it didn't take Ms. Rowling long to realize that she was not meant to be a secretary. Self described as "the worst secretary ever, very disorganized", she found it increasingly hard to remain attentive during meetings, actually writing story ideas instead of taking notes as she had been instructed.

When Ms. Rowling was 26 years old she moved to Portugal to be an English teacher. Ms. Rowling has been quoted many times as saying she loved teaching English, often teaching in the afternoons and evenings so that she could be free to work on her writing during the mornings. It was during this period that she began working on a story about a 'wizard".

Ms. Rowling met and married a journalist in Portugal (he was Portuguese), and her daughter Jessica was born in 1993. Shortly after the birth of her daughter, the marriage ended in divorce and Ms. Rowling, along with her infant daughter moved to Edinburgh, Scotland so that J K could be near her younger sister, Di.

It was during this time that Ms. Rowling became determined to not only finish her Harry Potter 'wizard' novel, but to get it published. Often she would write in restaurants, where she and her daughter could stay warm while she wrote.

Ms. Rowling requested a grant from the Scottish Arts Council, which she eventually received, in order to complete her book. When it was completed and after several rejections, Ms. Rowling sold the novel, Harry Potter and The Philosopher's Stone, to Bloomsbury in the UK for the equivalent of about $4,000.

To support her daughter and herself, Ms. Rowling began working as a French teacher. After several months Arthur A Levine Books/Scholastic Press bought the American rights to the first "Harry Potter", and Ms. Rowling received enough money to give up teaching and write full time. Ms. Rowling has described this moment as the happiest of her life.

After Bloomsbury Children's Books published the book in June 1997, it wasn't long before Ms. Rowling was recognized as a major discovery. The awards and accolades grew quickly for both Harry Potter and Ms. Rowling. In 1997 the book won The British Book Awards Children's Book of the Year, and the Smarties Prize.

When published in the US, in September of 1998, the book was renamed and released by Arthur A Levine Books / Scholastic Press; the new title was Harry Potter and the Sorcerer's Stone

Ms. Rowling quickly wrote a sequel, Harry Potter and The Chamber of Secrets, which was published July of 1998 in the UK, and in June 1999 in the USA. Immediately after this successful sequel a third book, Harry Potter and The Prisoner of Azkaban, was published in July and September of 1999, in the UK and the USA, respectively.

To her amazement, and joy, Ms. Rowling became a household name when the first three installments of the Harry Potter series took over the top 3 slots in the New York Times bestsellers list. (It's interesting to note that the books also did as well, achieving similar results, in the UK)

By the summer of 2000, Ms. Rowling had reportedly earned over $400 million for her first three Harry Potter books, which have been printed in 35 languages and sold over 30 million copies. Her fourth book in the popular series, entitled Harry Potter and the Goblet of Fire, pre-sold over one million advanced copies, with a first printing of 5.3 million.

Because of her domination and incredible success on the New York Times bestseller list, the decision was made to introduce a bestseller list for children's books, which would eliminate the dominating factor of these bestsellers on the current The New York Times bestseller list. This brought a tremendous amount of relief and happiness to a lot of competing authors - and a tremendous honor to Ms. J K Rowling.

Rowling's first book in the series, *Harry Potter and the Philosopher's Stone* (1997; U.S. title *Harry Potter and the Sorcerer's Stone*), was an immediate success, appealing to both children (its intended audience) and adults.

Featuring vivid descriptions and an imaginative story line, it followed the adventures of the unlikely hero Harry Potter, a lonely orphan who discovers that he is actually a wizard and enrolls in the Hogwarts School of Witchcraft and Wizardry.

The book received numerous awards, including the British Book Award. Succeeding volumes—*Harry Potter and the Chamber of Secrets* (1998), *Harry Potter and the Prisoner of Azkaban* (1999), *Harry Potter and the Goblet of Fire* (2000), *Harry Potter and the Order of the Phoenix* (2003), and *Harry Potter and the Half-Blood Prince* (2005)—also were best sellers, available in more than 200 countries and some 60 languages.

In 2001 the companion books *Fantastic Beasts & Where to Find Them* and *Quidditch Through the Ages* were published, with proceeds going to charity. The series sparked great enthusiasm among children and was credited with generating a new interest in reading.

A film version of the first Harry Potter book was released in 2001 and became one of the top-grossing movies in the world. Other volumes were also made into highly successful films.

Rowling was appointed OBE (Officer of the British Empire) in March 2001. Till date she has published seven "*Harry Potter*" series book, latest one being "*Harry Potter & The Deathly Hallows*" released in July, 2007.

JACK LONDON

Jack London was born in San Francisco. He was deserted by his father, "Professor" William Henry Chaney, an itinerant astrologer, and raised in Oakland by his mother Flora Wellman, a music teacher and spiritualist. London's stepfather John London, whose surname he took, was a failed storekeeper. London's youth was marked by poverty. At the age of ten he became an avid reader, and borrowed books from the Oakland Public Library, where Ina Coolbirth recommended him the works of Flaubert, Tolstoy and other major novelist.

After leaving school at the age of 14, London worked as a

seaman, rode in freight trains as a hobo and adopted socialistic views as a member of the protest armies of the unemployed.

In 1894 he was arrested in Niagara Falls and jailed for vagrancy. These years made him determined to raise himself out of poverty but they also gave later material for such works as *The Sea-Wolf* (1904), which was partly based on his horrific experiences as a sailor in the Pacific Ocean. *The Road* (1907), a collection of short stories, inspired later writers like John Steinbeck and Jack Kerouac.

Without having much formal education, London spent much time in public libraries reading fiction, philosophy, poetry, political science, and at the age of 19 gained admittance to the University of California in Berkeley. During this period he had already started to write. His first great love was Mabel Applegate, a middle-class girl, who became the model for Ryth Morse in *Martin Eden* (1909). Later London wrote to Anna Strunsky, the second love in his life: "Her virtues led her nowhere. Works? She had none.

Her culture was a surface smear, her deepest depth a singing shallow." London left the school before the year was over and went to seek a fortune in the Klondike gold rush of 1897. His attempt was unsuccessful. London spent the winter near Dawson City, suffering from scurvy. In the spring he returned to San Francisco his notebook full of plans for stories.

For the remainder of 1898 London again tried to earn his living by writing. His early stories appeared in the *Overland Monthly* and *Atlantic Monthly*. In 1900 he married Elisabeth (Bess) Maddern; their home became a battle field between Bess and London's mother Flora.

Three years later he left her and their two daughters, eventually to marry Charmian Kittredge, an editor and outdoorswoman. The marriage lasted until London's death. Charmian became the model of London's women characters, such as Paula in *The Little Lady of the Big House* (1916).

In 1901 London ran unsuccessfully on the Socialist party ticket for mayor of Oakland. He started to produce steadily novels, nonfiction, and short stories, becoming in his lifetime one of the most popular authors. London had early built his system of producing a daily quota of thousand words. He did not give up even during his travels and drinking periods.

London's first novel, *The Son of the Wolf*, appeared in 1900. By 1904 Jack London was the author of 10 books. *Son of the Wolf* gained a wide audience as his other Alaska stories, *The Call of the Wild* (1903), in which a giant pet dog Buck finds his survival instincts in Yukon, *White Fang* (1906), and *Burning Daylight* (1910).

"There is an ecstasy that marks the summit of life, and beyond which life cannot rise. And such is the paradox of living, this ecstasy comes when one is most alive, and it comes as a complete forgetfulness that one is alive.

This ecstasy, this forgetfulness of living, comes to the artist, caught up and out of himself in a sheet of flame; it comes to the soldier, war-mad on a stricken field and refusing quarter; and it came to Buck leading the pack, sounding the old wolf-cry, straining after the food that was alive and that fled swiftly before him through the moonlight." (from *The Call of the Wild*)

In 1902 London went to England, where he studied the backside of the British imperium: the living conditions in

East End and working class areas of the capital city. Originally he set out for South Africa to report the Boer War. His book about the economic degradation of the poor, *The People of the Abyss* (1903), was a surprise success in the U.S. but criticized in England.

London produced this classic of investigative reporting in seven weeks. In the middle of bitter separation in 1904, London traveled to Korea as a correspondent for Hearst's newspapers to cover the war between Russia and Japan (1904-05).

Next year he published his first collection of non-fiction pieces, *The War of the Classes*, which included his lectures on socialism. In 1907 London and Charmian started aboard the *Snark*, the author's self-designed ketch, a sailing trip around the world. On the voyage he began to write *Martin Eden*. After hardships - his captain was incompetent, the ketch was inefficient - they abrupted the journey in Australia. London's financial affairs were in chaos, his teeth gave him incessant pain, and he began to buy plots from a struggling writer, Sinclair Lewis, to produce more articles and stories for sale.

London had purchased in 1910 a large tract of land near Glen Ellen in Sonoma County, and devoted his energy and money improving and enlarging his Beauty Ranch. He also traveled widely and reported on the Mexican revolution. In 1913 London's Beauty Ranch, still incomplete, was destroyed by fire, and he was told by his doctor that his kidneys were failing. According to some sources, London's dream castle was burned deliberately - and it was uninsured.

Among London's major works are *The Sea-Wolf* (1904), remembered from its Nietzschean hero, visionary fantasy

The Iron Heel (1908), which became very popular in the Soviet Union, *The Cruise of the Snark* (1911), a travel book from his journeys in South Pacific, and semi-autobiographical *Martin Eden*, London's most autobiographical novel. "Being unaware of the needs of others, of the whole human collective need, Martin Eden lived only for himself, fought only for himself, and if you please, died for himself." The protagonist with the Biblical name is uneducated sailor, rough outsider, who aspires to money and status through his urge to write.

He is drawn to Ruth Morse, a woman who has everything he thinks he wants a wife to have - beauty, charm, wealth. Brissenden, Eden's Faustian friend, was modelled on George Sterling, a minor romantic poet and London's close colleague.

Eden gains success with his sea novel called *Overdue*. He becomes disillusioned, returns to the sea as a first-class passenger on the *Mariposa*, and commits suicide. "Perhaps Nietzsche had been right. Perhaps there was no truth in anything, no truth in truth - no such thing as truth," Eden thinks before his death. "And somewhere at the bottom he fell into darkness.

That much he knew. He had fallen into darkness. And at the instant he knew, he ceased to know." The book was considered by critics a failure, and London's literary reputation sank.

Burning Daylight (1910), an optimistic Klondike adventure story, was greeted as a return from his "sad phase of unrest". In *John Barleycorn* London revealed his own artistic exhaustion and drinking problems: "The things I had fought for and burned my midnight oil for had failed me. Success - I despised it. Recognition - it was dead ashes. Society, men and women above the rack and the much of the waterfront and the forecastle - I was appalled by their unlovely mental mediocrity.

Love of a woman - it was like all the rest. Money - I could sleep in only one bed at a time, and of what worth was an income of a hundred porter-houses a day when I could eat only one? Art, culture - in the face of the iron facts of biology such things were ridiculous, the exponents of such things only the more ridiculous." Politically London had come far from his earlyn idealism. Although he had begun his career as a Socialist, he did not support the Mexican freedom fighters, and took the side of American interests during the Mexican Revolution.

A few months before his death, London resigned from the Socialist Party. Debts, alcoholism, illness, and fear of losing his creativity darkened the author's last years. He died on November 22, 1916, officially of gastro-intestinal uremia.

However, there has been speculations that London committed suicide with morphine, but the two vials which were found did not contained the doses acquired for a suicide - especially for someone who was trained to take morphine against suffering. - "Jack London was never an original thinker.

He was a great gobbler-up of the world, physically and intellectually. He was the kind of writer who went to a place and wrote his dreams into it, who found an Idea and spun his psyche around it.

He was a workaday literary genius/hack who knew instinctively that Literature was a generous host, always having room for one more at her table." (L.E. Doctorow in *The New York Times*, December 11, 1988)

London's literary models were Kipling, Stevenson. He was also influenced by the theories of Darwin, Spencer, Marx, and Nietzsche. In his later years London read the works of Carl Jung. His influence has been considerable on such writers as Ernest Hemingway, Jack Kerouac, and Robert Ruark. Upton Sinclair has often been considered London's literary successor.

JANE AUSTEN

English writer, who first gave the novel its modern character through the treatment of everyday life. Although Austen was widely read in her lifetime, she published her works anonymously. The most urgent preoccupation of her young, well-bred heroines is courtship, and finally marriage. Austen's best-known books include *Pride and Prejudice* (1813) and *Emma* (1816). Virginia Woolf called her "the most perfect artist among women."

Jane Austen was born in Steventon, Hampshire, where her father was a rector. She was the second daughter and seventh child in a family of eight. The first 25 years of her life Austen spent in Hampshire. She was tutored at home. Her parents were avid readers and she received a broader education than many women of her time. On her father's retirement, the family moved to Bath.

Austen started to write for family amusement as a child. Her earliest-known writings date from about 1787. Very shy about her writing, she wrote on small pieces of paper that she slipped under the desk plotter if anyone came into the room.

After the death of her father in 1805, she lived with her mother and sister in Southampton and moved in 1809 to a large cottage in the village of Chawton. Austen never married, but her social life was active. She was connected with the middling-rich landed gentry that she portrayed in her novels.

In Chawton Austen started to write her major works, among them *Sense and Sensibility*, the story of the impoverished Dashwood sisters, Marianne and Elinor, who try to find proper husbands to secure their social position. The novel was written in 1797 as the revision of a sketch called *Elinor and Marianne*, composed when the author was 20.

Austen's heroines are determined to marry wisely and well, but romantic Marianne is a character who feels intensely about everything and loses her heart to an irresponsible seducer. "*I could not be happy with a man whose taste did not in every point coincide with my own.*

He must enter into all my feelings; the same with books, the same music must charm us both." Reasonable Elinor falls in love with a gentleman already engaged. "'*I have frequently detected myself in such kind of mistakes," said Elinor, "in a total misapprehension of character in some point or another: fancying people so much more gay or grave, or ingenious or stupid than they really are, and I can hardly tell why or in what the deception originated.*

Sometimes one is guided by what they say of themselves, and very frequently by what other people say of them, without giving oneself time to deliberate and judge.'"

In all of Austen's novels her heroines are ultimately married. *Pride and Prejudice* described the clash between Elisabeth Bennet, the daughter of a country gentleman, and Fitzwilliam Darcy, a rich aristocratic landowner. Their relationship starts from dislike but at last they fall in love and are happily united.

In 1998 appeared a sequel to the novel, entitled *Desire and Duty*, written by Teddy F. Bader, et al. It followed the ideas Jane Austen told her family. *Emma* was written in comic tone and told the story of Emma Woodhouse, who finds her destiny in marriage. During the story Emma, a snobbish young woman, develops into someone capable of feeling and love.

Austen focused on middle-class provincial life with humor and understanding. She depicted the life of minor landed gentry, country clergymen and their families, in which marriage mainly determined women's social status.

Most important for her were those little matters, as Emma says, "on which the daily happiness of private life depends." Although Austen restricted to family matters, and she passed the historical events of the Napoleonic wars, her wit and observant narrative touch has been inexhaustible delight to readers. Of her six great novels, four were published anonymously during her lifetime. At her death on July 18, 1817 in Winchester, Austen was writing the unfinished *Sanditon*. Austen was buried in Winchester Cathedral.

Austen's brother Henry made her authorship public after her death. *Emma* had been reviewed favorably by Sir Walter

Scott, who wrote in his journal of March 14, 1826: Austen had a talent for describing the involvements and feelings and characters of ordinary life which is to me the most wonderful I have ever met with.

The Big Bow-Wow strain I can do myself like any now going; but the exquisite touch, which renders ordinary commonplace things and characters interesting, from the truth of the description and the sentiment, is denied to me." Charlotte Brontë and E.B. Browning found her limited. It was not until the publication of J.E. Austen-Leigh's *Memoir* in 1870 that a Jane Austen cult began to develop. Austen's unfinished *Sanditon* was published in 1925.

JOHN KEATS

Keats had a tragically short life; yet even though he died so young the beauty that shines through his work is remarkable by any standards.

He was born on the 31st October 1795, in Finsbury. His father was the principal servant at the Swan and Hoop stables, who married the daughter of his master. His mother appears to have been a tall, bright young woman fond of the pleasures of this life. There were four children, John being the oldest, born prematurely at seven months.

By the age of twelve, John Keats had lost both of his parents. There was some money left for the four children, and they got about £2,000 pounds each. John was sent to a school at

Enfield. He earned a reputation for some fighting ability, but gained all the prizes for English literature. He showed a keen interest in Greek mythology, and this can be seen in some of his later work.

At the age of fourteen his guardian apprenticed him to a surgeon, a Mr. Thomas Hammond, in Edmonton, near Enfield, for two hundred guineas and expenses. He didn't much care for this, for it did not interest him as poetry did. Still, he had little choice in the matter.

He came to London to enter St. Thomas' Hospital as a student, and had the good fortune to meet Leigh Hunt. There was a small coterie of young writers, and with their encouragement, he began to concentrate on his literary aspirations. These began to engross him and he soon gave up his medical work.

At the age of twenty-two he issued his first little volume. It appears to have pleased none but his friends. Yet it contained many gems, fondly quoted nowadays, (e.g. *"Born of the very sigh that silence heaves"*).

Written within a period of but a few years, the earlier work naturally showed some immaturity, and indeed attracted somewhat harsh criticism from those who were his inferiors; but his work then developed into exquisite jewels of the English language that confounded his critics.

His longest work, Endymion, was prefaced by an apology for what he perceived were its inadequacies. It was published in 1818, when he was at Teignmouth, Devon. He had then only a few years to live. The simple opening lines have passed into the English language as a precious sequence of words, often quoted:

A thing of beauty is a joy forever:
Its loveliness increases; it will never
Pass into nothingness; .....".

In these days of ballpoint pens and word processors, it is difficult to appreciate the labour involved in composing and putting down on paper such a long piece. The lighting, too, was meagre by modem standards, and makes Keats' work all the more formidable.

The lovely contradictory phrase *"Heard melodies are sweet, but those unheard are sweeter,"* appears in his Ode to a Grecian Urn. *"Season of mists and mellow fruitfulness"* opens his Ode to Autumn, written whilst on a brief visit to Winchester.

These and many others are part of the happy legacy of this young man. Few poets could have produced so many oft quoted phrases. Everywhere, those who speak English have a rich treasury of words and expressions that can be recalled with great pleasure.

In his early years his outlook with regard to women was disdainful, almost hostile; but then he became attracted to a Miss Cox, a cousin of his friend J.H. Reynolds.

This did not lead to anything. Nevertheless, his outlook was still one of some scorn with regard to love of women. He wrote that he found such to be *"a cloying treacle to the wings of independence"*.

However, as with most young men, this attitude was to change completely. He fell deeply in love with a lady called Fanny Brawne, (later to marry and become Mrs. Lindon) and some thirty-seven letters he wrote her have survived. He was consumed with love for her, and at the same time beginning to suffer the strain of the consumption that was to kill him.

It has been suggested that his passion for Fanny aggravated his illness, the double strain of his romantic desires and his disease leading to an earlier death than might otherwise have occurred.

However that might be, Keats was aware of his condition, and the threat to his life. Consumption was not an uncommon illness in those days, and when it developed there was little hope. It was a scourge among all classes of society, and the doctors were impotent. For most sufferers a diagnosis of tuberculosis was a notice of death.

It is reported that in February 1820, noting the blood he had coughed up, after a cold trip on the coach, he called for a candle that he might distinguish the colour. Examining the stain, he said that it was arterial blood, and stated calmly that it was his death warrant.

He knew, as did people generally, that consumption was a killer, and there was no cure. Sufferers were advised to travel to areas where the air was purer, and this could alleviate the distress a little; but there were no drugs to combat the disease. Switzerland had many clinics, and was the favourite place where doctors used to send their patients.

Shelley invited him to Pisa, but Keats declined. He set out on a voyage to warmer climes, and suffered a very rough passage in the Bay of Biscay. His great friend Severn tended him devotedly during his last days, travelling with him, nursing him, and watching over him with great affection till death claimed him on February 23rd, 1821.

Some ten days earlier the poet had asked that on his grave should be placed the words *"Here lies one whose name was writ in water"*. He was buried in the Protestant Cemetery at Rome.

Only twenty-six years old when he died, yet Keats left us odes, sonnets, stanzas, and longer works that have become immortal.

English literature is a rich field for warm enjoyment, and John Keats has an honoured place in it.

JOHN MILTON

John Milton was born in London. His mother Sarah Jeffrey was the daughter of a merchant sailor, and his father had risen to prosperity as a scrivener or law writer - he also composed music. The family was wealthy enough to afford a second house in the country.

Milton was educated at St Paul's School and then at Christ's College, Cambridge (1625-32), where he was called, half in scorn, "The Lady of Christ's." During his Cambridge period, while considering himself destined for the ministry, he began to write poetry in Latin, Italian, and English. He was expelled for a term after starting a fist fight with his tutor.

On leaving Cambridge Milton had given up his original plan to become a priest. He adopted no profession but spent six years at leisure in his father's home, writing during that time *L'Allegro, Il Penseroso* (1632), *Comus* (1634), and *Lycidas* (1637). In 1635 the Miltons moved to Horton, Buckinghamshire, where John pursued his studies in Greek, Latin, and Italian.

He traveled in France and Italy in the late 1630s, meeting in Paris the jurist and theologian Hugo Grotius and the astronomer Galileo Galilei in Florence - there are references to Galileo's telescope in *Paradise Lost.* His conversation with the blind scientist Milton recorded in *Areopagitica*, which attacked censorship. Milton returned to London in 1639, and set up a school with his nephews and a few others as pupils.

The Civil War silenced his poetic work for 20 years. War divided the country as Oliver Cromwell fought against the king, Charles I.

Concerned with the Puritan cause, Milton wrote a series of pamphlets against episcopacy (1642), on divorce (1643), in defense of the liberty of the press (1644), and in support of the regicides (1649). He also served as the secretary for foreign languages in Cromwell's government.

After the death of Charles I, Milton published *The Tenure of Kings and Magistrates* (1649) supporting the view that the people had the right to depose and punish tyrants.

In 1651 Milton became blind, but like Jorge Luis Borges is our century, blindness helped to stimulate his verbal richness. *"He sacrificed his sight, and then he remembered his first desire, that of being a poet,"*. Borges wrote in one of his lectures. After the Restoration of Charles II in 1660, he was arrested as a noted defender of the Commonwealth, but was soon released.

Besides public burning of *Eikonklastes* and the first *Defensio* in Paris and Toulouse, Milton escaped from more punishment after Restoration, but he became a relatively poor man. In the 1660s Milton moved with his third wife to what is now Burnhill Row. He spent there the remaining years of his life, apart from a brief visit to Chalfont St Giles in 1665, to avoid the plague. His late poems were dictated to his daughter, nephews, friends, disciples, and paid amanuenses.

Milton was married three times (Mary Powell, 1642; Katherine Woodcock, 1656; Elizabeth Minshull, 1662). His marriages were unhappy. Mary Powell grew bored with the life of a poet soon after the honeymoon was over and went back home where she stayed for three years. Milton wrote his famous essays on divorce.

In *The Doctrine and Discipline of Divorce* (1643) Milton argued that a true marriage was of mind as well as of body, and that the chaste and modest were more likely to find themselves 'chained unnaturally together' in unsuitable unions than those who had in youth lived loosely and enjoyed more varied experience.

Though Milton was Puritan, morally austere and conscientious, some of his religious beliefs were unconventional to the point of heresy, and came into conflict with the official Puritan stand.

"By labor and intent study (which I take to be my portion in this life), joined with the strong propensity of nature, I might perhaps leave something so written to after-times, as they should not willingly let it die." (from The Reason of Church Government, 1641)

Milton died from 'gout struck in' on November 8, 1674 in Chalfont, St. Giles, Buckinghamshire. He was buried beside his father in St Giles', Cripplegate. Many writers believe that Milton's grave was desecrated when the church was undergoing repairs. All the teeth and 'a large quantity of the hair' were taken as souvenirs by grave robbers.

As a writer, Milton's towering figure was recognized early, but his personality and works have continued to arouse discussion. Even T.S. Eliot has attacked the author and described him as one whose sensuousness had been 'withered by book-learning.' Eliot claimed that Milton's poetry 'could *only* be an influence for the worse.'

The theme of Fall and expulsion from Eden in *Paradise Lost* had been in Milton's mind from 1640s. His ambition was to compose an epic poem to rival the works of ancient writers, such as Homer and Virgil.

The poem was originally issued in 10 books in 1667, and in 12 books in the second edition of 1674. The troubled times, in which Milton lived, left their mark on his theme of religious conflict.

Paradise Lost is not easy to read with its odd syntax, difficult vocabulary, and complex, noble style. It tells a biblical story of Adam and Eve, with God, and Lucifer (Satan), who is thrown out of Heaven to corrupt humankind. Satan, the most beautiful of the angels, is at his most impressive: he wakes up, on a burning lake in Hell, to find himself surrounded by his stunned followers. He has been defeated in the War of Heaven.

"All is not lost; th' unconquerable Will,

And study of revenge, immortal hate,

And courage never to submit or yield... ".

Milton created a powerful and sympathetic portrait of Lucifer. This view influenced deeply Romantic poets William Blake and Percy Bysshe Shelley, who saw Satan as the real hero of the poem and a rebel against the tyranny of Heaven.

In *The Marriage of Heaven and Hell* Blake stated that Milton as 'a true Poet, and of the Devil's party without knowing it.' Many other works of art have been inspired by *Paradise Lost*, among them Joseph Haydn's oratorio *The Creation*, Alexander Pope's *The Rape of the Lock* and *The Dunciad*, John Keat's poem *Endymion*, Lord Byron's *The Vision of Judgment*, satanic Sauron in J.R.R. Tolkien's saga *The Lord of the Rings.*

KALIDASA

An Indian poet and dramatist, Kalidasa lived sometime between the reign of Agnimitra, the second Shunga king (c. 170 BC) who was the hero of one of his dramas, and the Aihole inscription of AD 634 which praises Kalidasa's poetic skills. Most scholars now associate him with the reign of Candra Gupta II (reigned c. 380-c. 415).

Little is known about Kalidasa's life. According to legend, the poet was known for his beauty which brought him to the attention of a princess who married him.

However, as legend has it, Kalidasa had grown up without much education, and the princess was ashamed of his ignorance and coarseness.

A devoted worshipper of the goddess Kali (his name means literally Kali's slave), Kalidasa is said to have called upon his goddess for help and was rewarded with a sudden and extraordinary gift of wit. He is then said to have become the most brilliant of the "nine gems" at the court of the fabulous king Vikramaditya of Ujjain. Legend also has it that he was murdered by a courtesan in Sri Lanka during the reign of Kumaradasa.

Kalidasa's first surviving play, Malavikagnimitra or Malavika and Agnimitra tells the story of King Agnimitra, a ruler who falls in love with the picture of an exiled servant girl named Malavika.

When the queen discovers her husbands passion for this girl, she becomes infuriated and has Malavika imprisoned, but as fate would have it, Malavika is in fact a true-born princess, thus legitimizing the affair.

Kalidasa's second play, generally considered his masterpiece, is the Shakuntala which tells the story of another king, Dushyanta, who falls in love with another girl of lowly birth, the lovely Shakuntala.

This time, the couple is happily married and things seem to be going smoothly until Fate intervenes. When the king is called back to court by some pressing business, his new bride unintentionally offends a saint who puts a curse on her, erasing the young girl entirely from the king's memory.

Softening, however, the saint concedes that the king's memory will return when Shakuntala returns to him the ring he gave her. This seems easy enough—that is, until the girl loses the ring while bathing. And to make matters worse, she soon discovers that she is pregnant with the king's child. But true love is destined to win the day, and when a fisherman finds the ring, the king's memory returns and all is well. Shakuntala is remarkable not only for it's beautiful love poetry, but also for its abundant humor which marks the play from beginning to end.

The last of Kalidasa's surviving plays, Vikramorvashe or Urvashi Conquered by Valor, is more mystical than the earlier plays. This time, the king (Pururavas) falls in love with a celestial nymph named Urvashi. After writing her mortal suitor a love letter on a birch leaf, Urvashi returns to the heavens to perform in a celestial play.

However, she is so smitten that she misses her cue and pronounces her lover's name during the performance. As a punishment for ruining the play, Urvashi is banished from heaven, but cursed to return the moment her human lover lays eyes on the child that she will bear him.

After a series of mishaps, including Urvashi's temporary transformation into a vine, the curse is eventually lifted, and the lovers are allowed to remain together on Earth. Vikramorvashe is filled poetic beauty and a fanciful humor that is reminiscent of Shakespeare's A Midsummer Night's Dream.

In addition to his plays, Kalidasa wrote two surviving epic poems Raghuvamsha ("Dynasty of Raghu") and Kumarasambhava ("Birth of the War God"), as well as the lyric "Meghaduta" ("Cloud Messenger"). He is generally considered to be the greatest Indian writer of any epoch.

LEO TOLSTOY

Leo Tolstoy (1828-1910). Leo Tolstoy had written in his diary, "My life is some stupid and spiteful joke that someone has played on me." And now he was dying. His last words were, "This is the end . . . and it doesn't really matter."

He died of pneumonia on November 20, 1910. During his long life, Count Leo Tolstoy had been much more than the "angry young man" who turns novelist in order to change things or to better the condition of the oppressed.

He was a tormented man, and his mind was plagued by the things he had done. "I put men to death," he wrote in his voluminous diary. "I fought duels to slay others, I lost at cards, wasted my substance wrung from the sweat of peasants, punished the latter cruelly, and deceived men. Lying, robbery, drunkenness, violence, murder . . . all committed by me, not one crime omitted." In other words, he had done all of the things that people expected young Russian noblemen to do, only he had a conscience and worried about it.

These thoughts, combined with his overwhelming fear of dying, drove him to the verge of madness and suicide many times.

Leo Tolstoy, the author of what critics have called 2 great complete pictures of society, War and Peace and Anna Karenina, was born at his mother's ancestral home, Vasnaya Polyana. His parents had died by the time he was 10, and for much of the next 20 years he roamed the countryside gambling recklessly, drinking to excess, and, as he put it, "rioting with all sorts of loose women."

He contracted syphilis and gonorrhea, and although his many faults (sexual and otherwise) tore at his brain, he never failed to take advantage of an opportunity to carouse when it was offered.

Tolstoy's earliest recollection was of pushing an older woman off the front porch of Vasnaya Polyana for unrequited love. He was 5 and the "older woman" was 10.

This older woman grew up to be the mother of the hotheaded and quarrelsome girl named Sofia whom Tolstoy married on September 23, 1862. Not wishing to hide anything from his new bride, Count Tolstoy promptly showed the new Countess Tolstoy his diary, which was filled to the brim with shocking confessions and the sordid details of his wild younger days.

He was 34 and she was only 18, but they were married anyway. Seventeen years and 13 children later, Leo Tolstoy was so depressed that he was again seriously considering suicide, but something happened that changed his entire outlook on life.

He read the Sermon on the Mount and realized that the teachings of Christ were the key to happy living and, for Leo Tolstoy, to adopt an opinion was to act. He promptly tried to give his estate to the poor, throw his money to the peasants, and place his published works in the public domain for all the peoples of the world.

His wife, who now had to support their 13 children in addition to handcopying his manuscripts (War and Peace was copied 7 times in its entirety), said No. But that didn't stop Tolstoy from putting on peasants' rags and working in the fields every day from sunup to sundown.

A conniving leech named Chertkov was drawn to the "new Master Tolstoy," and not only urged him to ignore his wife's pleadings but suggested that he go even further in his quest for the perfect and happy life.

The solution was to give up everything to a deserving peasant . . . namely to Chertkov himself. The gullible Tolstoy drew up a new will leaving his estate to Chertkov. That was the last straw for the already enraged Countess Tolstoy.

When Leo caught her foraging through his papers in search of the will, he decided to leave Russia and all of his worries behind him.

It was a cold night in October when Leo Tolstoy boarded the overcrowded, poorly heated, 3rd-class train for the Russian border. He caught pneumonia and died in a blaze of publicity one month later. When he was 5 years old, Leo had told his brother that he knew of a secret that would destroy all the evil in men, and this secret was buried under a little green stick near Vasnaya Polyana. His brother buried him under the little green stick near their family home.

LEWIS CARROLL

Lewis Carroll (Charles Lutwidge Dodgson) (1832-1898). On July 4, 1862, 2 young English scholars took 3 little girls on a picnic. One of the men was Charles Lutwidge Dodgson, and during this outing he told a fascinating tale of a girl named Alice and what happened to her after she fell down a rabbit hole.

It was not unusual for Dodgson to tell stories, for he was very fond of little girls and liked to entertain them. However, on this occasion he outdid himself and so enraptured his listeners that one of them, Alice Liddell, the model for the heroine of the story, insisted that he write it down.

That night in his room at Oxford University he worked furiously until 6 in the morning, adding incidents to flesh out the story. He illustrated the work with his own drawings and presented it to Alice, who was not the only one enchanted with the result.

For Henry Kingsley, a Victorian novelist and friend of Alice's family, happened to read Alice's Adventures Underground and told Mrs. Liddell that he thought highly of the book and that she should urge the author to publish it.

Dodgson took this advice, but before he had his work published he very wisely decided to replace his drawings with those of the famous illustrator, John Tenniel. A more fortunate union of writer and artist could not be imagined, for in 1865 their combined efforts brought forth a book—retitled Alice's Adventures in Wonderland—that has become one of the most famous children's books of all time, one that appeals to child and adult alike. (A curious sidelight is that Dodgson, dissatisfied with the 1st printing, stopped the presses after 48 copies had been run off.

Twenty one of these have survived and are among the rarest of rare books.) On the title page of Alice appeared a pen name that has become immortal—Lewis Carroll.

This cleric and mathematician chose to hide behind a pseudonym because he wished to keep his "nonsense" works separate from his mathematical and other treatises to which he attached his true name. He arrived at "Lewis Carroll" by reversing his 1st and middle names, translating them into Latin (Ludovicus Carolus), and then retranslating into English.

This perfectly illustrates the playful mind of a man who delighted in puzzles, riddles, and the most elaborate word play.

He has added a number of words to the English language, like "chortle" and "galumph" (a triumphant gallop), and his poems and poetic parodies have often been anthologized. Alice's Adventures in Wonderland and its successor, Through the Looking-Glass and What Alice Found There, are among the most often quoted works in the language.

Not only was Dodgson a brilliant man of letters; he was also an exceptional photographer. He was noted for his portraits of leading Victorians, and he specialized in studies of nude children, particularly girls.

This latter activity caused some eyebrows to be raised, and he abruptly ceased taking pictures altogether. Some have tried to find sinister things in Dodgson's affection for little girls, but perhaps the true cause of his lifelong pursuit of preadolescent females was a lonely bachelor's need for love. He found at least one grown-up woman attractive, the actress Ellen Terry.

Their relationship managed to make up in endurance what it lacked in intimacy. Perhaps, as have many of his readers, he found in his world of "nonsense" a refuge from the real world.

LOUISA MAY ALCOTT

American author, known for her children' books, especially *Little Women* (1868). Unknown to her family and the public, Alcott begun writing 'rubbish novels', sometimes anonymously, sometimes as 'A.N. Barnard', to contribute to the family income.

Alcott was born in Germantown (now part of Philadelphia). During her childhood her family moved to Boston. She spent most of her life in the Boston-Concord area, and received almost all her early education from her father Bronson Alcott (1799-1888), who was member of the New England Transcendentalists.

He was an idealistic, if impractical person, who bvelieved in the spiritual life, as contrasted wirh the material life. When a visiting English author criticized her father's teaching methods, the schoolmaster Alcott moved with his family to Concord.

Among the family friends were Theodore Parker, Henry David Thoreau, and Ralph Waldo Emerson. Alcott began to keep diary at the age of seven. Her first book, *Flower Fables* (1854), a collection of tales, was originally written for Emerson's daughter Ellen.

After the failure of her father's utopian community *Fruitlands*, she took care with her mother of the welfare of the family. Her mother, who had not been so enthusiastic about the New Eden plan of her husband, took in boarder, when the family moved into Boston again.

By 1860 both her short stories and poems began to appear in the *Atlantic Monthly* (now *The Atlantic*).

As an ardent abolitionist she volunteered in the American Civil War as a nurse and served in 1862-1863 at the Union Hospital in Georgetown, D.C. During this time Alcott contracted typhoid from which she never completely recovered.

In 1863 Alcott published her letters in book form under the title *Hospital Sketches*. The work was well received and encouraged her to continue with her writing aspirations.

Alcott's first novel, *Moods*, was published in 1867. In the same year she became editor of a children's magazine, *Merry Museum*. With the publication of *Little Women*, which started under the pressure of financial need, Alcott gained enormous fame as a writer. Responding to her publisher's request, she draw her material from her own family and from the New England milieu where she had grown up.

The novel was followed by several other popular works, among them *Good Wives* (1869), *Old-Fashioned Girl* (1870), and *Little Men* (1871). Alcott's last years were shadowed by the the deaths of her mother and her sister May, who left behind a little daughter. Alcott died in Boston on March 6, 1888.

MARK TWAIN

Mark Twain was born in Florida, Missouri on 30 November 1835, the sixth child born to Jane Lampton (1803-1890) and John Marshall Clemens (1798-1847). In 1839 the Twain family moved to their Hill Street home, now the Mark Twain Boyhood Home and Museum with its famous whitewashed fence, in the bustling port city of Hannibal, Missouri. Situated on the banks of the Mississippi river it would later provide a model for the fictitious town of St. Petersburg in *Huckleberry Finn* and *Tom Sawyer.*

When Twain's father died in 1847 the family was left in financial straits, so eleven year old Samuel left school (he was in grade 5) and obtained his first of many jobs working with various newspapers and magazines including the *Hannibal Courier* as journeyman printer. *"So I became a newspaperman. I hated to do it, but I couldn't find honest employment."* He also started writing, among his first stories "A Gallant Fireman" (1851) and "The Dandy Frightening the Squatter" (1852).

After traveling to and working in New York and Philadelphia for a few years he moved back to St. Louis in 1857. It was here that the lure of the elegant steamboats and festive crowds drew his attention and he became an apprentice 'cub' river pilot under Horace Bixby, earning his license in 1858. As a successful pilot plying his trade between St. Louis and New Orleans, Twain also grew to love the second longest river in the world which he describes affectionately in his memoir *Life on the Mississippi* (1883).

"The face of the water, in time, became a wonderful book — a book that was a dead language to the uneducated passenger, but which told its mind to me without reserve, delivering its most cherished secrets as clearly as if it uttered them with a voice. And it was not a book to be read once and thrown aside, for it had a new story to tell every day."

An important part of a river pilot's craft is knowing the waters and depths, which, for the mighty Mississippi and her reefs, snags, and mud are ever changing. To 'mark twain' is to sound the depths and deem them safe for passage, the term adopted by Clemens as his pen name in 1863. In 1858 his brother Henry died in an explosion on the steamboat *Pennsylvania*.

Life on the river would provide much fodder for Twain's future works that are at times mystical, often sardonic and witty, always invaluable as insight into the human condition.

With the outbreak of Civil War in 1861 passage on the Mississippi was limited, so at the age of twenty-six Twain moved on from river life to the high desert valley in the silver mining town of Carson City, Nevada with his brother Orion, who had just been appointed Secretary of the Nevada Territory. He had never traveled out of the state but was excited to venture forth on the stagecoach in the days before railways, described in his semi-autobiographical novel *Roughing It* (1872).

Twain tried his hand at mining on Jackass Hill in California in 1864, and also began a prolific period of reporting for numerous publications including the *Territorial Enterprise*, *The Alta Californian*, *San Francisco Morning Call*, *Sacramento Union* and *The Galaxy*. He traveled to various cities in America, met Frederick Douglass, Harriet Beecher Stowe and Charles Dickens in New York, and visited various countries in Europe, Hawaii, and the Holy Land which he based *Innocents Abroad* (1869) on. Short stories from this period include "Advice For Little Girls" (1867) and "The Celebrated Jumping Frog of Calavaras County" (1867).

In 1870 Twain married Olivia 'Livy' Langdon (1845-1904) with whom he would have four children. Three died before they reached their twenties but Clara (1870-1962) lived to the age of eighty-eight. The Twain's home base was now Hartford, Connecticut, where in 1874 Twain built a home, though they traveled often. Apart from numerous short stories he wrote during this time and *Tom Sawyer*, Twain also collaborated on *The Gilded Age* (1873) with Charles Dudley Warner.

A Tramp Abroad (1880), Twain's non-fiction satirical look at his trip through Germany, Italy, and the Alps and somewhat of a sequel to *Innocents Abroad* was followed by *The Prince and the Pauper* (1882). Hank Morgan, time traveler in *A Connecticut Yankee in King Arthur's Court* (1889) reflects Twain's friendship with pioneering inventor and electrical engineer Nikola Tesla and interest in scientific inventions. Twain also continued to uphold a busy lecture series throughout the United States. In 1888 he was awarded an honorary Master of Art degree from Yale University.

For some years Twain had lost money in various money making schemes like mining, printing machines, the Charles L. Webster Publishing Co., and The Mark Twain Self-Pasting Scrap Book though he never lost his sense of humour.

In 1892, friend and fellow humorist and author Robert Barr, writing as 'Luke Sharp' interviewed Twain for *The Idler* magazine that he owned with Jerome K. Jerome. Twain's novel *The American Claimant* (1892) was followed by *The Tragedy of Pudd'Nhead Wilson* (1894), first serialized in *Century Magazine.*

Tom Sawyer Abroad (1894) was followed by *Tom Sawyer, Detective* in 1896. His favourite fiction novel, *Personal Recollections of Joan of Arc* (1896) was first serialised in *Harper's Magazine.* By 1895, unable to control his debts, he set off on a world lecture tour to Australia, Canada, Ceylon, India, New Zealand, and South Africa to pay them off.

Following the Equator (1897) is his travelogue based on his tour, during which he met Mahatma Gandhi, Sigmund Freud, and Booker T. Washington.

With another successful lecture tour under his belt and now much admired and celebrated for his literary efforts, Mark, Livy and their daughter Jane settled in New York City. Yale University bestowed upon him an honorary Doctor of Letters degree in 1901 and in 1907 he was awarded an honorary Doctor of Letters by Oxford University. The same year *A Horse's Tale* and *Christian Science* (1907) were published. While traveling in Italy in 1904, Livy died in Florence.

For Twain's 70th birthday on 30 November 1905 he was fêted at Delmonico's restaurant in New York, where he delivered his famous birthday speech, wearing his trademark all-year round white suit.

That year he was also a guest of American President Theodore 'Teddy' Roosevelt at the White House and addressed the congressional committee on copyright issues.

He was also working on his biography with Albert Bigelow Paine. His daughter Jane became very sick and was committed to an institution, but died in 1909 of an epileptic seizure. In 1908 Twain had moved to his home 'Stormfield' in Redding, Connecticut, though he still actively traveled, especially to Bermuda.

Mark Twain died on 21 April 1910 in Redding, Connecticut and now rests in the Woodlawn Cemetery in Livy's hometown of Elmira, New York State, buried beside her and the children.

A memorial statue and cenotaph in the Eternal Valley Memorial Park of Los Angeles, California states: "Beloved Author, Humorist, and Western Pioneer, This Original Marble Statue Is The Creation Of The Renowned Italian Sculptor Spartaco Palla Of Pietrasanta."

Twain suffered many losses in his life including the deaths of three of his children, and accumulated large debts which plagued him for many years, but at the time of his death he had grown to mythic proportions as the voice of a spirited and diverse nation, keen observer and dutiful reporter, born and died when Halley's Comet was visible in the skies.

"Death, the only immortal who treats us all alike, whose pity and whose peace and whose refuge are for all—the soiled and the pure, the rich and the poor, the loved and the unloved." —Twain's last written statement

MIRZA GHALIB

Mirza Asadullah Beg Khan — known to posterity as Ghalib, a 'nom de plume' he adopted in the tradition of all classical Urdu poets, was born in the city of Agra, of parents with Turkish aristocratic ancestry, probably on December 27th, 1797. As to the precise date, Imtiyaz Ali Arshi has conjectured, on the basis of Ghalib's horoscope, that the poet might have been born a month later, in January 1798.

The question of Ghalib's early education has often confused Urdu scholars. Although any record of his formal education that might exist is extremely scanty, it is also true that Ghalib's circle of friends in Delhi included some of the most eminent minds of his time. There is, finally, irrevocably, the evidence of his writings, in verse as well as in prose, which are distinguished not only by creative excellence but also by the great knowledge of philosophy, ethics, theology, classical literature, grammar, and history that they reflect.

In or around 1810, two events of great importance occured in Ghalib's life: he was married to a well-to-do, educated family of nobles, and he left for Delhi. One must remember that Ghalib was only thirteen at the time. It is impossible to say when Ghalib started writing poetry.

Perhaps it was as early as his seventh or eight years. On the other hand, there is evidence that most of what we know as his complete works were substantially completed by 1816, when he was 19 years old, and six years after he first came to Delhi.

In Delhi Ghalib lived a life of comfort, though he did not find immediate or great success. He wrote first in a style at once detached, obscure, and pedantic, but soon thereafter he adopted the fastidious, personal, complexly moral idiom which we now know as his mature style.

It is astonishing that he should have gone from sheer precocity to the extremes of verbal ingenuity and obscurity, to a style which, next to Meer's, is the most important and comprehensive styles of the *ghazal* in the Urdu language before he was even twenty.

The course of his life from 1821 onward is easier to trace. His interest began to shift decisively away from Urdu poetry to Persian during the 1820's, and he soon abandoned writing in Urdu almost altogether, except whenever a new edition of his works was forthcoming and he was inclined to make changes, deletions, or additions to his already existing opus.

Ghalib was never really a part of the court except in its very last years, and even then with ambivalence on both sides. There was no love lost between Ghalib himself and Zauq, the king's tutor in the writing of poetry; and if their mutual dislike was not often openly expressed, it was a matter of prudence only.

There is reason to believe that Bahadur Shah Zafar, the last Moghul king, and himself a poet of considerable merit, did not much care for Ghalib's style of poetry or life.

There is also reason to believe that Ghalib not only regarded his own necessary subservient conduct in relation to the king as humiliating but he also considered the Moghul court as a redundant institution. Nor was he well-known for admiring the king's verses. However, after Zauq's death Ghalib did gain an appiontment as the king's advisor on matters of versification.

He was also appointed, by royal order, to write the official history of the Moghul dynasty, a project which was to be titled "Partavistan" and to fill two volumes.

The one volume "Mehr-e-NeemRoz", which Ghalib completed is an indifferent work, and the second volume was never completed, supposedly because of the great disturbances caused by the Revolt of 1857 and the consequent termination of the Moghul rule. Possibly Ghalib's own lack of interest in the later Moghul kings had something to do with it.

The only favourable result of his connection with the court between 1847 and 1857 was that he resumed writing in Urdu with a frequency not experienced since the early 1820's. Many of these new poems are not panegyrics, or occasional verses to celebrate this or that. He did, however, write many *ghazals* which are of the same excellence and temper as his early great work.

Infact, it is astonishing that a man who had more or less given up writing in Urdu thirty years before should, in a totally different time and circumstance, produce work that is, on the whole, neither worse nor better than his earlier work. One wonders just how many great poems were permanently lost to Urdu when Ghalib chose to turn to Persian instead.

In its material dimensions, Ghalib's life never really took root and remained always curiously unfinished. In a society where almost everybody seems to have a house of his own, Ghalib never had one and always rented one or accepted the use of one from a patron. He never had books of his own, usually reading borrowed ones.

He had no children; the ones he had, died in infancy, and he later adopted the two children of Arif, his wife's nephew who died young in 1852. Ghalib's one wish, perhaps as strong as the wish to be a great poet, that he should have a regular, secure income, never materialized. His brother Yusuf, went mad in 1826, and died, still mad, in that year of all misfortunes, 1857.

His relations with his wife were, at best, tentative, obscure and indifferent. Given the social structure of mid-nineteenth-century Muslim India, it is, of course, inconceivable that *any* marriage could have even begun to satisfy the moral and intellectual intensities that Ghalib required from his relationships; given that social order, however, he could not conceive that his marriage could serve that function.

And one has to confront the fact that the child never died who, deprived of the security of having a father in a male-oriented society, had had looked for material but also moral certainities — not certitudes, but certainities, something that he can stake his life on. So, when reading his poetry it must be remembered that it is the poetry of more than usually vulnerable existence.

Ghalib had many attitudes toward the British, most of them complicated and quite contradictory. His diary of 1857, the "Dast-Ambooh" is a pro-British document, criticizing the British here and there for excessively harsh rule but expressing, on the whole, horror at the tactics of the resistance forces. His letters, however, are some of the most graphic and vivid accounts of British violence that we possess.

We also know that "Dast-Ambooh" was always meant to be a document that Ghalib would make public, not only to the Indian Press but specifically to the British authorities. And he even wanted to send a copy of it to Queen Victoria. His letters, are to the contrary, written to people he trusted very much, people who were his friends and would not divulge their contents to the British authorities.

As Imtiyaz Ali Arshi has shown (at least to my satisfaction), whenever Ghalib feared the intimate, anti-British contents of his letters might not remain private, he requested their destruction, as he did in the case of the Nawab of Rampur. I think it is reasonable to conjecture that the diary, the "Dast-Ambooh", is a document put together by a frightened man who was looking for avenues of safety and forging versions of his own experience in order to please his oppressors, whereas the letters, those private documents of one-to-one intimacy, are more real in the expression of what Ghalib was in fact feeling at the time. And what he was feeling, according to the letters, was horror at the wholesale violence practised by the British.

Yet, matters are not so simple as that either. We cannot explain things away in terms of altogether honest letters and an altogether dishonest diary. Human and intellectual responses are more complex. The fact that Ghalib, like many other Indians at the time, admired British, and therefore Western, rationalism as expressed in constitutional law, city planning and more.

His trip to Calcutta (1828-29) had done much to convince him of the immediate values of Western pragmatism. This immensely curious and human man from the narrow streets of a decaying Delhi, had suddenly been flung into the broad, well-planned avenues of 1828 Calcutta — from the aging Moghul capital to the new, prosperous and clean capital of the rising British power, and, given the precociousness of his mind, he had not only walked on clean streets, but had also asked the fundamental questions about the sort of mind that planned that sort of city. In short, he was impressed by much that was British.

The years between 1857 and 1869 were neither happy nor very eventful ones for Ghalib. During the revolt itself, Ghalib remained pretty much confined to his house, undoubtedly frightened by the wholesale massacres in the city.

Many of his friends were hanged, deprived of their fortunes, exiled from the city, or detained in jails. By October 1858, he had completed his diary of the Revolt, the "Dast-Ambooh", published it, and presented copies of it to the British authorities, mainly with the purpose of proving that he had not supported the insurrections.

Although his life and immediate possesions were spared, little value was attached to his writings; he was flatly told that he was still suspected of having had loyalties toward the Moghul king. During the ensuing years, his main source of income continued to be the stipend he got from the Nawab of Rampur. "Ud-i-Hindi", the first collection of his letters, was published in October 1868. Ghalib died a few months later, on February 15th, 1869.

O. HENRY

O. Henry was born William Sydney Porter in Greenboro, North Carolina. His father, Algernon Sidney Porter, was a physician. When William was three, his mother died, and he was raised by his parental grandmother and paternal aunt. William was an avid reader, but at the age of fifteen he left school, and then worked in a drug store and on a Texas ranch.

He continued to Houston, where he had a number of jobs, including that of bank clerk. After moving in 1882 to Texas, he worked on a ranch in LaSalle County for two years. In 1887 he married Athol Estes Roach; they had one daughter and one son.

'It was beautiful and simple as all truly great swindles are." (from The Octopus Marooned')

In 1894 Porter started a humorous weekly *The Rolling Stone*. It was at this time that he began heavy drinking. When the weekly failed, he joined the *Houston Post* as a reporter and columnist. In 1894 cash was found to have gone missing from the First National Bank in Austin, where Porter had worked as a bank teller. When he was called back to Austin to stand trial, Porter fled to Honduras to avoid trial. Little is known about Porter's stay in Central America.

It is said, that he met one Al Jennings, and rambled in South America and Mexico on the proceeds of Jenning's robbery. After hearing news that his wife was dying, he returned in 1897 to Austin. In 1897 he was convicted of embezzling money, although there has been much debate over his actual guilt. Porter entered in 1898 a penitentiary at Columbus, Ohio.

While in prison, Porter started to write short stories to earn money to support his daughter Margaret. His first work, 'Whistling Dick's Christmas Stocking' (1899), appeared in *McClure's Magazine*.

The stories of adventure in the U.S. Southwest and in Central America gained an immediately success among readers. After doing three years of the five years sentence, Porter emerged from the prison in 1901 and changed his name to O. Henry. According to some sources, he acquired the pseudonym from a warder called Orrin Henry.

It also could be an abbreviation of the name of a French pharmacist, Eteinne-Ossian Henry, found in the U.S. Dispensatory, a reference work Porter used when he was in the prison pharmacy.

O. Henry moved to New York City in 1902 and from December 1903 to January 1906 he wrote a story a week for the New York *World*, also publishing in other magazines. Henry's first collection, *Cabbages and Kings*, appeared in 1904. The second, *The Four Million*, was published two years later and included his well-known stories 'The Gift of the Magi' and 'The Furnished Room'.

The Trimmed Lamp (1907) explored the lives of New Yorkers and included 'The Last Leaf' - the city itself Henry liked to call 'Bagdad-on the-Subway.' In one of his stories, 'One Dollar's Worth', O. Henry deals with the judicial system. Judge Derwent receives a letter from an ex-convict, in which the writer, 'Rattlesnake' threatens his daughter and the district attorney, Littlefield.

A young Mexican, Rafael Ortiz, is accused of passing a counterfeit silver dollar, made principally of lead. Rafael's girl, Joya Treviñas, tells Littlefield that he is innocent - she was sick, and needed medicine, and that was the reason why Rafael used the dollar. Littlefield refuses to help, and Joya says that "it the life of the girl you love is ever in danger, remember Rafael Ortiz."

When he drives out of the town with Nancy Derwent, they meet Mexico Sam, the writer of the letter. He starts to shoot them from distance with his rifle. Littlefield can't hurt him with his own gun which has only tiny pellets.

Then he remembers Joya's words, and manages hit Mexico Sam, who falls from his horse dead as a rattlesnake. Next morning in the court he tells: "'I shot him,' said the district attorney, 'with Exhibit A of your counterfeiting case. Lucky thing for me - and somebody else - that it was as bad money as it was! It sliced up into slugs very nicely. Say, Kil, can't you go down to the jacals and find where that Mexican girl lives? Miss Derwent wants to know.'"

Henry's best known work is perhaps the much anthologized 'The Ransom of Red Chief' (see Howard Hawks and Nunnally Johnson), published in the collection *Whirligigs* in 1910. O. Henry's humorous, energetic style shows the influence of Mark Twain and Ambrose Bierce.

The story tells about two kidnappers, who make off with the young son of a prominent man. They find out that the child is a real nuisance. In the end they agree to pay the boy's father to take him back. - "Sam," says Bill, "I suppose you'll think I'm a renegade. but I couldn't help it.

I'm a grown person with masculine proclivities and habits of self-defense, but there is a time when all systems of egotism and predominance fail. The boy is gone. I sent him home. All is off. There was martyrs in old times," goes on Bill, "that suffered death rather than give up the particular graft they enjoyed. None of 'em ever was subjugated to such supernatural tortures as I have been. I tried to be faithful to our articles of depredation; but there came a limit."

Heart of the West (1907) presented western stories, of which 'The Last of the Troubadours' J. Frank Dobie named "the best range story in American fiction." 'The Caballero's Way' featured as a character the Cisco Kid. During his life time, O. Henry published 10 collections and over 600 short stories. His last years were shadowed by alcoholism, ill health, and financial problems.

He was a fast writer, like the Russian Anton Checkhov (1860-1904), but drinking on average two quarts of whiskey daily, did not improve the quality of his work. In 1907 O. Henry married Sara Lindsay Coleman, also born in Greensboro. The marriage was not happy, and they separated a year later. O. Henry died of cirrhosis of the liver on June 5, 1910, in New York. Three more collections, *Sixes and Sevens* (1911), *Rolling Stones* (1912) and *Waifs and Strays* (1917), appeared posthumously. In 1918 the O. Henry Memorial Awards were established to be given annually to the best magazine stories, the winners and leading contenders to be published in an annual volume.

OMAR KHAYYAM

Omar Kayyam was born Ghiyath al-Din Abul Fateh Omar Ibn Ibrahim al-Khayyam in Nishapur, the capital of Khurasan. The commercially rich province was at that time under Seljuq rule.

Little is known of Omar's early life. The epithet Khayyam signifies "tent-maker" - it is possible that Omar or his father, Ibrahim the Tentmaker, one time exercised that trade. Omar was educated at his native town, where he studied under the celebrated teacher, the Iman Mowaffak. In Samara he completed his treatise on algebra. When the Seljuq Sultan Malik Shah offered him preferment at court, Omar made a request: "The greatest boon you can confer on me," he said, "is to let me live in a corner under the shadow of your fortune, to spread wide the advantages of Science, and pray for your long life and prosperity." (from *Rubaiyat of Omar Khayyam*, trans. by Edward Fitzgerald, 1859)

The Vizier Nizam al-Mulk granted Omar a pension, which enabled him to devote himself to learning and research, especially in mathematics and astronomy. In 1074 he was invited to undertake astronomical research.

Omar was also commissioned to build an observatory in the city of Isfahan in collaboration with other astronomers. Malik Shah appointed him a member of a group of eight scholars assigned to reform the Moslem calendar, a task comparable to Pope Gregorius XIII's revision of the Julian calendar. Their work inaugurated the Jalalaean or Seljuq era, beginning March 15, 1079. Omar's revision of the old Persian solar calendar was discontinued when Islamic orthodoxy gained power, but in 1925 it was again introduced in Iran.

Omar's series of astronomical tables is known as *Ziji Malikshahi*. Among his other mathematical writings are a work on algebra and a study of *The Difficulties of Euclid's Definitions* (1077). He tried to classify equations of the first degree and his algebra textbook, dealing with quadric and cubic equations in particular, was very advanced compared to contemporary European studies of mathematics.

In the West Omar's reputation as a poet has shadowed his achievements as a mathematician. His poems were made popular by Edward Fitzgerald, who translated his *Rubaiyat* (quatrains) from the original Persian to English. The first edition was published anonymously. It contained 101 *rubáiyát* (or *rubáis*).

Only 250 copies were printed and soon forgotten. Fitzgerald arranged the scattered quatrains in long, continuous elegy. His work was more than an ordinary translation, it was so inspired and visionary, that some critics later believed that it was an English poem with Persian allusions. The "exotic" verses caught the attention of Rossetti and Swinburne, who wrote that Fitzgerald "has given to Omar Khayyam a permanent place among the major English poets".

The second edition of the work in 1868 marked the beginning of Omar Khayyam cult. "Isaac Luria the Lion taught that the soul of a dead man can enter an unfortunate soul to nourish or instruct it," wrote the Argentinian writer Jorge Luis Borges, "perhaps, around 1857, Omar's soul took up residence in Fitzgerald's." (in 'The Enigma of Edward Fitzgerald', 1951) Omar's *rubáiyát* did not circulate in his homeland during his lifetime. Also contemporary biographers did not note him as a great poet.

According to convention, in quatrains the first, second and last lines are rhymed, while the third line rarely follows the rhyme of the other lines. Thus a *rubái* (plural *rubáiyát*) has the form *aaba.* Each line expresses a complete thought.

Omar Khayyam, whose daily thoughts in his *rubáiyát* were often pessimistic and who was troubled by eternal question of life, death, deity, and the nature of the universe, was viewed with suspicion by orthodox Muslims. For his philosophy he was "said to have been especially hated and dreaded by the Sufis, whose Practise he ridiculed" (G. Fitzgerald). However, the Sufi poets read his works and the *rubáiyát* in general were frequently sung at mystical concerts.

The thoughts of Avicenna (980-1037) and Omar were condemned by the highly influential Islamic philosopher Abu

Hamid al-Ghazali (1058-1111) in *Incoherence of the Philosophers.* Al-Ghazali saw that the Muslim Aristotelian and Neoplatonic philosophers were is many questions in conflict with the fundamentals of religion.

Major themes in Omar's *rubáiyát* is the fragility of human life. The pleasures of Paradise do not give any comfort for the poet - "Cash is better than a thousand promises." Although he has solved "all the puzzles of the Universe", he cannot loosen the "fetter of death". Omar also praised wine - "Drink wine - it drives sorrow from the heart." The subject was inflammable, because wine and drunkenness was prohibited by the principles of Islamic law.

However, these poems could be interpreted metaphorically, referring to spiritual or romantic intoxication." *Drink either at the company of wise, Or with your beloved at the moonrise,*" Omar wrote. He called wine the water of life; we are rare bowls made by the cosmic potter - "*The cup is the body, its wine is the soul.*"

After the death of his patron, Nizam al-Mulk, in 1092, Omar went on a pilgrimage to Mecca. In one poem, assigned to Omar, the poet wrote: *"Khayyám, who stitched the tents of science,* Has fallen in grief's furnace and been sudden burned; *The shears of Fate have cut the tent ropes of his life,* And the broker of Hope has sold him for nothing." After returning to Nishapur, he continued as a teacher and reluctantly made some astrological predictions. Like Avicenna, he was skeptical of astrology.

According to an anecdote, Omar said to one of his pupils, with whom he held conversations in a garden: "My tomb shall be in a spot where the north wind may scatter roses over it." Omar Khayyam died on December 4, 1131 in Nishapur. 'Ali ibn Zaidu'l-Baihaqi wrote in his biography, that Omar was reading Avicenna's *Book of Healing.*

He then called his household to hear his will and last instructions, and said before his death: "Oh Lord, I have known You according to the sum of my ability. Pardon me since verily my knowledge is my recommendation to You." 'Ali ibn Zaid's book, which appeared sometime between 1158 and 1170, has the oldest biographical notice on Omar.

Forty-five years after Omar's death appeared a work, in which his verses were described as "a tissue of error like poisonous snakes" in the eyes of the Canon Law *(News of the Learned with Reports of the Sages* by Al-Qifri, abridged by Az-Zausani in 1249).

Omar's poetry is preserved only in mutilated manuscripts, and not much of his prose writings have survived. The problem of whether or not Omar composed all the poem attributed to him, including the famous quatrain with the words "A Jug of Wine, a Loaf of Bread - and Thou", has been hard to solve. A.J. Avberry, who used 13th-century manuscripts, identified at least 250 authentic poems.

Perhaps the most complete is the one in the library of the Asiatic Society, Calcutta. The manuscript contains 516 quatrains. Other important manuscripts are in the Chester Beatty collection and at Cambridge.

OSCAR WILDE

Oscar Wilde (*Oscar Fingal O'Flahertie Wills Wilde*) was born in Dublin on 16 October 1854 to Sir William Wilde and his wife Jane. Oscar's mother, Lady Jane Francesca Wilde (1820-1896), was a successful poet and journalist. She wrote patriotic Irish verse under the pseudonym "Speranza".

Oscar's father, Sir William Wilde (1815 - 1876), was a leading ear and eye surgeon, a renowned philanthropist and gifted writer who wrote books on archaeology and folklore. Oscar had an elder brother, Willie, and a younger sister, Isola Francesca, who died at the early age of 10.

Oscar Wilde was educated at Portora Royal School,

Enniskillen, County Fermanagh (1864-71), Trinity College, Dublin (1871-74) and Magdalen College, Oxford (1874-78). While at Oxford, he became involved in the aesthetic movement and became an advocate for 'Art for Art's Sake' (*L'art pour l'art*). Whilst at Magdalen, he won the 1878 Newdigate Prize for his poem Ravenna.

After he graduated, he moved to Chelsea, in London (1879), to establish a literary career. In 1881, he published his first collection of poetry - 'Poems' that received mixed reviews by critics. He worked as art reviewer (1881), lectured in the United States and Canada (1882), and lived in Paris (1883). He also lectured in Britain and Ireland (1883 - 1884). From the mid-1880s he was regular contributor for Pall Mall Gazette and Dramatic View.

On May 29, 1884, Oscar married Constance Lloyd (died 1898), daughter of wealthy Queen's Counsel Horace Lloyd. They had two sons, Cyril (1885) and Vyvyan (1886). To support his family, Oscar accepted a job as the editor of Woman's World magazine, where he worked from 1887-1889. In 1888 he published The Happy Prince and Other Tales, fairy-stories written for his two sons. His first and only novel, The Picture of Dorian Gray, was published in 1891 and recieved quite a negative response.

This had much to do with the novel's homoerotic overtones, which caused something of a sensation amongst Victorian critics. In 1891 Wilde began an affair with Lord Alfred Douglas, nicknamed 'Bosie', who became both the love of his life and his downfall.

Wilde's marriage ended in 1893. Wilde's greatest talent was for writing plays, his first play, 'Lady Windermere's Fan,' opened in February 1892. He produced a string of extremely popular comedies including 'A Woman of No Importance' (1893), 'An Ideal Husband (1895)' and 'The Importance of Being Earnest' (1895). These plays were all highly acclaimed and firmly established Oscar as a playwright.

In April 1895, Oscar sued Bosie's father for libel as the Marquis of Queensberry had accused him of homosexuality. Oscar's case was unsuccessful and he was himself arrested and tried for gross indecency. He was sentenced to two years hard labor for the crime of sodomy. During his time in prison he wrote De Profundis, a dramatic monologue and autobiography, which was addressed to Bosie.

Upon his release in 1897, he wrote "The Ballad of Reading Gaol", revealing his concern for inhumane prison conditions. He spent the rest of his life wandering Europe, staying with friends and living in cheap hotels. He died of cerebral meningitis on November 30, 1900, penniless, in a cheap Paris hotel.

PREMCHAND

Premchand brought realism to Hindi literature. Premchand wrote on the realistic issues of the day-communalism, corruption, zamindari, debt, poverty, colonialism etc. He avoided the use of highly Sanskritized Hindi and instead used the dialect of the common people.

Premchand popularly known as Munshi Premchand was one of the greatest literary figures of modern Hindi literature. His stories vividly portrayed the social scenario of those times.

Premchand's real name was Dhanpat Rai Srivastava. He was born on July 31, 1880 in Lamahi near Varanasi where his father Munshi Azaayab Lal was a clerk in the post office. Premchand lost his mother when he was just seven years old. His father married again. Premchand was very close to his elder sister.

His earliest schooling was in Persian and Urdu with a Maulvi in a village nearby. Later, he joined an English school in the city and passed his Enterance examination in 1898. When he was studying in the ninth class he was married, much against his wishes. He was only fifteen years old at that time.

Premchand lost his father when he was sixteen years old. Premchand was left responsible for his stepmother and stepsiblings. He earned five rupees a month tutoring a lawyer's child. Premchand passed his matriculation exam with great effort and took up a teaching position, with a monthly salary of eighteen rupees.

He passed his intermidiate and B.A. examinations as a private student years later while in service. He took up a teacher's job in a private school at Chunar (Off Mirzapur) shortly after he passed his Enterance examination. After one academic year at Chunar, he joined government service and taught at various places in Uttar Pradesh for twenty-one years.

In 1910, he was hauled up by the District Magistrate in Jamirpur for his anthology of short stories Soz-e-Watan (Dirge of the Nation), which was labelled seditious. His book Soz-e-Watan was banned by the then British government, which burnt all of the copies.

Initially Premchand wrote in Urdu under the name of Nawabrai. However, when his novel Soz-e-Watan was confiscated by the British, he started writing under the pseudonym Premchand.

Before Premchand, Hindi literature consisted mainly of fantasy or religious works. Premchand brought realism to Hindi literature. He wrote over 300 stories, a dozen novels and two plays. The stories have been compiled and published as Maansarovar. His famous creations are: Panch Parameshvar, Idgah, Shatranj Ke Khiladi, Poos Ki Raat, Bade Ghar Ki Beti, Kafan, Udhar Ki Ghadi, Namak Ka Daroga, Gaban, Godaan, and Nirmala.

Premchand was a great social reformer; he married a child widow named Shivarani Devi. She wrote a book on him, Premchand Gharmein after his death. In 1921 he answered Gandhiji's call and resigned from his job.

He worked to generate patriotism and nationalistic sentiments in the general populace. When the editor of the journal _Maryaada_ was jailed in the freedom movement, Premchand worked for a time as the editor of that journal. Afterward, he worked as the principal in a school in the Kashi Vidyapeeth.

The main characteristic of Premchand's writings is his interesting storytelling and use of simple language. His novels describe the problems of rural and urban India. He avoided the use of highly Sanskritized Hindi and instead used the dialect of the common people. Premchand wrote on the realistic issues of the day -communalism, corruption, zamindari, debt, poverty, colonialism etc.

Premchand's writings have been translated not only into all Indian languages, but also Russian, Chinese, and many other foreign languages. He died on October 8, 1936.

RABINDRANATH TAGORE

ONE of the greatest writer in modern Indian literature, Bengali poet, novelist, educator, and an early advocate of Independence for India. Tagaore won the Nobel Prize for Literature in 1913. Two years later he was awarded the knighthood, but he surrendered it in 1919 as a protest against the Massacre of Amritsar, where British troops killed some 400 Indian demonstrators. Tagore's influence over Gandhi and the founders of modern India was enormous.

Rabindranath Tagore was born in Calcutta into a wealthy and prominent Brahman family. His father was Maharishi Debendranath Tagore, a religious reformer and scholar. His mother, Sarada Devi, died when Tagore was very young - he realized that she will never come back was when her body was carried through a gate to a place where it was burned. Tagore's grandfather had established a huge financial empire for himself. He helped a number of public projects, such as Calcutta Medical College.

The Tagores tried to combine traditional Indian culture with Western ideas; all the children contributed significantly to Bengali literature and culture. However, in *My Reminiscences* Tagore mentions that it was not until the age of ten when he started to use socks and shoes.

And servants beat the children regularly. Tagore, the youngest, started to compose poems at the age of eight. Tagore's first book, a collection of poems, appeared when he was 17; it was published by Tagore's friend who wanted to surprise him.

Tagore received his early education first from tutors and then at a variety of schools. Among them were Bengal Academy where he studied history and culture. At University College, London, he studied law but left after a year - he did not like the weather.

Once he gave a beggar a gold coin - it was more than the beggar had expected and he returned it. In England Tagore started to compose the poem 'Bhagna Hridaj' (a broken heart).

In 1883 Tagore married Mrinalini Devi Raichaudhuri, with whom he had two sons and three daughters. In 1890 Tagore moved to East Bengal (now Bangladesh), where he collected local legends and folklore. Between 1893 and 1900 he wrote seven volumes of poetry, including SONAR TARI (The Golden Boat), 1894 and KHANIKA, 1900.

This was highly productive period in Tagore's life, and earned him the rather misleading epitaph 'The Bengali Shelley.' More important was that Tagore wrote in the common language of the people. This also was something that was hard to accept among his critics and scholars.

Tagore was the first Indian to bring an element of psychological realism to his novels. Among his early major prose works are CHOKHER BALI (1903, Eyesore) and NASHTANIR (1901, The Broken Nest), published first serially. Between 1891 and 1895 he published forty-four short stories in Bengali periodical, most of them in the monthly journal *Sadhana*.

Especially Tagore's short stories influenced deeply Indian Literature. 'Punishment', a much anthologized work, was set in a rural village. It describes the oppression of women through the tragedy of the low-caste Rui family.

Chandara is a proud, beautiful woman, "buxom, well-rounded, compact and sturdy," her husband, Chidam, is a farm-laborer, who works in the fields with his brother Dukhiram. One day when they return home after whole day of toil and humiliation, Dukhiram kills in anger his sloppy and slovenly wife because his food was not ready. To help his brother, Chidam's tells to police that his wife struck her sister-in-law with the farm-knife. Chandara takes the blame on to herself. 'In her thoughts, Chandara was saying to her husband, "I shall give my youth to the gallows instead of you. My final ties in this life will be with them."' Afterwards both Chidam and Dukhiram try to confess that they were quilty but Chandara is convicted. Just before the hanging, the doctor says that her husband wants to see her. "To hell with him," says Chandara.

In 1901 Tagore founded a school outside Calcutta, Visva-Bharati, which was dedicated to emerging Western and Indian philosophy and education. It become a university in 1921. He produced poems, novels, stories, a history of India, textbooks, and treatises on pedagogy. Tagore's wife died in 1902, next year one of his daughters died, and in 1907 Tagore lost his younger son.

Tagore's reputation as a writer was established in the United States and in England after the publication of GITANJALI: SONG OFFERINGS, about divine and human love. Tagore's poems were also praised by Ezra Pound, and drew the attention of the Nobel Prize committee. "There is in him the stillness of nature. The poems do not seem to have been produced by storm or by ignition, but seem to show the normal habit of his mind. He is at one with nature, and finds no contradictions.

And this is in sharp contrast with the Western mode, where man must be shown attempting to master nature if we are to have "great drama." (Ezra Pound in *Fortnightly Review*, 1 March 1913) However, Tagore also experimented with poetic forms and these works have lost much in translations into other languages.

Much of Tagore's ideology come from the teaching of the Upahishads and from his own beliefs that God can be found through personal purity and service to others. He stressed the need for new world order based on transnational values and ideas, the "unity consciousness." "The soil, in return for her service, keeps the tree tied to her; the sky asks nothing and leaves it free."

Politically active in India, Tagore was a supporter of Gandhi, but warned of the dangers of nationalistic thought. Unable to gain ideological support to his views, he retired into relative solitude. Between the years 1916 and 1934 he travelled widely. From his journey to Japan in 1916 he produced articles and books. In 1927 he toured in Southeast Asia. *Letters from Java*, which first was serialized in *Vichitra*, was issued as a book, JATRI, in 1929. His Majesty, Riza Shah Pahlavi, invited Tagore to Iran in 1932. On his journeys and lecture tours Tagore attempted to spread the ideal of uniting East and West.

While in Japan he wrote: "The Japanese do not waste their energy in useless screaming and quarreling, and because there is no waste of energy it is not found wanting when required. This calmness and fortitude of body and mind is part of their national self-realization."

Tagore wrote his most important works in Bengali, but he often translated his poems into English. At the age of 70 Tagore took up painting. He was also a composer, settings hundreds of poems to music.

Many of his poems are actually songs, and inseparable from their music. Tagore's 'Our Golden Bengal' became the national anthem of Bangladesh. Only hours before he died on August 7, in 1941, Tagore dictated his last poem. His written production, still not completely collected, fills nearly 30 substantial volumes.

RUDYARD KIPLING

Rudyard Kipling was born in Bombay, India, where his father, John Lockwood Kipling, was an arts and crafts teacher at the Jeejeebhoy School of Art. His mother, the former Alice Macdonald, was a sister-in-law of the painter Edward Burne-Jones.

India was at that time ruled by the British. Ruddy, as Kipling was affectionally called, was brought up by an *ayah*, who taught him Hidustani as his first language.

Oh, East is East, and West is West, and never the twain shall meet,
Till Earth and Sky stand presently at God's great Judgment Seat;
But there is neither East nor West, Border, nor Breed, nor Birth,

When two strong men stand face to face, tho' they come from the ends of the earth! (from 'The Ballad of East and West')

Kipling's writings at the age of thirteen were influenced by the pre-Raphaelites - and he also had family connections to them: two of his mother's sisters were married into the pre-Raphaelite community.

At the age of six he was taken to England by his parents and left for five years at a foster home at Southsea. Kipling, who was not accustomed to traditional English beatings, expressed later his feeling of the treatment in the short story 'Baa Baa, Black Sheep', in the novel *The Light That Failed* (1890), and in his autobiography (1937).

In 1878 Kipling entered United Services College, a boarding school in North Devon. It was an expensive institution that specialized in training for entry into military academies. His poor eyesight and mediocre results as a student ended hopes about military career. However, these years Kipling recalled in lighter tone in one of his most popular books, *Stalky & Co.* (1899).

Kipling's bookishness separated him from the other students; he had to wear glasses and was nicknamed "Gigger", for gig (carriage) for lamps. However, Kipling wrote about the non-conformist Headmaster, Cormell Price: "Many of us loved the Head for what he had done for us, but I owed him more than all of them put together and I think I loved him even more than they did."

Kipling returned to India in 1882, where he worked as a journalist in Lahore for *Civil and Military Gazette* (1882-87) and an assistant editor and overseas correspondent in Allahabad for *Pioneer* (1887-89). The stories written during his last two years in India were collected in *The Phantom Rickshaw.*

It that included the famous story 'The Man Who Would Be a King.' In the story a white trader, Daniel Dravot sets himself up as a god and king in Kafristan, but a woman discovers that he is a human and betrays him. His companion, Peachey Carnehan, manages to escape to tell the tale, but Dravot is killed.

Kilping's short stories and verses gained success in the late 1880s in England, to which he returned in 1889, and was hailed as a literary heir to Charles Dickens.

When he toured Japan he criticized the Japanese middle-class for its eagerness to adopt western fashions and values. "... I was a barbarian, and no true Sahib," he wrote. Between the years 1889 and 1892, Kipling lived in London and published *Life's Handicap* (1891), a collection of Indian stories that included 'The Man Who Was,' and *Barrack-Room Ballads*, a collection of poems that included 'Gunga Din,' a praise of a Hindu water carrier for a British Indian regiment. Wellington had viewed the private soldier as "the very scum of the earth", but Kipling portrayed him as the embodiment of British virtue.

In 1892 Kipling married Caroline Starr Balestier, the sister of an American publisher and writer, with whom he collaborated a novel, *The Naulahka* (1892). The young couple moved to the United States. Kipling was dissatisfied with the life in Vermont, and after the death of his daughter, Josephine, Kipling took his family back to England and settled in Burwash, Sussex. According to the author's sister, Kipling became a "harder man" - but also his political beliefs started to stiffen. Kipling's marriage was not in all respects happy.

The author was dominated by his wife who had troubles to accept all aspects of her husband's character. During these restless years Kipling produced *Many Inventions* (1893), *Jungle Book* (1894), a collection of animal stories for children, *The Second Jungle Book* (1895), and *The Seven Seas* (1896).

Widely regarded as unofficial poet laureate, Kipling refused this and many honors, among them the Order of Merit. During the Boer War in 1899 Kipling spent several months in South Africa. In 1902 he moved to Sussex, also spending time in South Africa, where he was given a house by Cecil Rhodes, the influential British colonial statesman. In 1901 appeared *Kim*, widely considered Kipling's best novel. The story, set in India, depicted adventures of an orphaned son of a sergeant in an Irish regiment.

Soon after Kipling had received the Nobel Prize, his output of fiction and poems began to decline. In 1923 Kipling published *The Irish Guards in the Great War*, a history of his son's regiment. Between the years 1922 and 1925 he was a rector at the University of St. Andrews. Kipling died on January 18, 1936 in London, and was buried in Poet's Corner at Westminster Abbey. Kipling's autobiography, *Something of Myself*, appeared posthumously in 1937.

Kipling did his best to obtain and destroy letters he had sent - to protect his private life. His widow continued the practice but a number of his letters survived and have been published. In 1884 he wrote to Edith Macdonald about his visit to an Afghan Khan, Kizil Bas, who had to stay in Lahore as a prisoner - the Afghan Sirdars had fought against the British.

The Khan asks Kipling to write to his "Khubber-Ke-Kargus" (newspaper) and help him to gain again his freedom. He throws a bundle of money to Kipling who refuses to take them. Then the Khan offers a Cashmiri girl, and Kipling loses his temper. Finally he promises three beautiful horse. Kipling resists the temptation, they smoke, drink coffee, and Kipling rides of the city. *"I haven't told anyone here of the bribery business because, if I did, some unscrupulous beggar might tell the Khan that he would help him and so lay hold of the money, the lady or, worse still, the horses. Besides I may able to help the old boy respectably and without any considerations."*

Kipling's glorification of the "Empire and extension" gained its peak in the poem 'The White Man's Burden' (1899): *"Take up the White Man's burden - / Send forth the best ye breed - / Go bind your sons to exile / To serve your captives' need; / To wait in heavy harness / On fluttered folk and wild - / Your new-caught, sullen peoples, / Half devil and half child."* George Orwell, who also spent his early childhood in India, rejected in an essay in *New English Weekly* (1936) Kipling's view of the world, which he associated with the ignorant and sentimental side of imperialism, but admired the author as a storyteller.

However, readers loved Kipling's romantic tales about the adventures of Englishmen in strange and distant parts of the world. Characteristic for Kipling is sympathy for the world of children, satirical attitude toward pompous patriotism, and belief in the blessings and superiority of the British rule, without questioning its basic nature.

SAINT KABIR DAS

Sant Kabir is considered to be one of the greatest poets as well as mystics ever born in India. He believed that human beings are equal and being one with God is the ultimate aim of every individual. His love and devotion towards the Supreme One clearly reflects in his poetry.

The Holy Guru Granth Sahib contains over 500 verses by the great saint, Kabir. The verses or dohas of Guru Kabir are still read by people with awe and admiration. Read on to explore the biography of Sant Kabir further.

He was as is widely acknowledged born in Year 1398 A.D.

Kabirpanthis (followers of Kabir) say that he lived upto the age of 120 years and give date of his death as 1518, but relying on the research of Hazari Prased Dwivedi, a British Scholar Charlotte Vaudenville is inclined to lend credence to these dates and has prooven that 1448 is probably the correct date of Saint Kabir's demise.

Kabir lived in the fifteenth Century after Christ, which was a time of great political upheaval in India. As is true of many contemporary religious teachers, very little reliable information concerning Kabir's life is available, though there is no dearth of legend gathering around him.

Kabir's life was centred around Kashi, also called Banaras (Varanasi) Legend has it that he was actually the son of a Brahmin widow who abandoned him and that he was found by a Muslim weaver named Niru, who adopted the boy and taught him the weaver's trade. It is not clear whether he ever married, but tradition gives him a wife named Loi and two children. His caste was that of Julaha and from his sayings his caste's heriditary occupation of weaving.

On the basis of modern research, it seems probable that Kabir belonged to a family of non-celibate yogis converted, not long before and to a considerable degree superficially to Islam. From the writings of Kabir it seems that his knowledge of Islam was slight, rather in his poetical utterances (Bani) a wealth of Hathayoga terminology and a thought structure which bears obvious resemblance to Nath Yogis.

Nath Yogis in addition to the yogic conception that all truth is experimental, i.e. to be realized within the body with the aid of psycho-physical practices, concentration, control of breathing and thus making the body incorruptible and the yogis immortal.

Bhakti movement was started by hindu saints while Sufi mysticism by Muslim saints in medieval India (1200-1700). Kabir immensely contributed to the Bhakti Movement and is considered a pioneer of Bhakti along with Ravidas, Farid, and Namdev. His concept of love as a path of suffering may possibly indicate, in some measure, a debt to the Sufis. These and other elements from Nath tradition, bhakti and sufism, kabir combined with his own mystical nature and produced synthesis which is the distinctive religion of Kabir. Tradition tells us that Swami Ramanand was his Guru (a teacher).

In fifteenth century, Benaras was the seat of Brahmin orthodoxy and their learning center. Brahmins had strong hold on all the spheres of life in this city. Thus Kabir belonging to a low caste of Julaha had to go through immense tough time of preaching his idealogy. Kabir and his followers would gather at one place in the city and meditate. Brahmins ridiculed him for preaching to prostitutes and other low castes.

Kabir satirically denounced Brahmins and thus won hearts of people around him. There is no doubt that single most famous important person from the city of Benaras today is none other than Saint Kabir. Kabir through his couplets not only reformed the mindset of common villagers and low caste people but give them self confidence to question Brahmins.

It was 100 years after him that Tulsidas broke the hegemony of Brahmins by writing Ram Charitra Manas, a poem of Ramayana at Benaras which went against the tradition of Brahmins.

Kabir was in fact first person to go against Brahmins and be so successfull. Benaras was devasted by an attack by a Muslim invader Tamur Lang or "Tamur the lame" during his time. Kabir also denounced mullahs and their rituals of bowing towards kaba five times a day. Because of open condemnation of established and popular religoins, Kabir became an object of the wrath of both Hindus and Muslims in and around Benaras.

Kabir travelled in and around Benaras to preach his beliefs. Kabir believed in sell-surrender and God's bhakti. The Kabirpanthis follow a lite of singing the praises of God, prayers and a simple and pure life of devotion.

Kabir recommends ceaseless singing of God's praises. He virtually suggests withdrawal from the world. He is against al1 ritualistic and ascetic methods as means to salvation. It is true that Kabir refers to some yogic terms in describing the meditational and mystic methods of the yogis. But, there is no ground to suggest that he himself recommends the yogic path. In fact, far from recommending yoga, he is quite strong in condemning ascetic or yogic methods, and says that yogis, in their meditations, become prey to maya. The point wil1, however be considered further while comparing Radical bhakti with Nathism.

The moral tone is quite strong in Kabir's hymns. "Kabir deck thyself with garments of love. Love them is given honour whose body and soul speak the truth." "The ruby of goodness is greater than all thc mines of rubies, all the wealth of three worlds resides in the goodness of heart.

When thc wealth of contentment is won, all other wealth is as dust." "Where there is mercy, there is strength, where there is forgivenesss there is He." "The man who is kind and practises righteousness, who remains passive in the aftairs of the world, who considers creatures of the world as his own self, he attains the immortal Being; the true God is ever with him. Kabir suggests inward worship and remembrance of God. For him, true worship is only inwards. Put on the rosary inward. By counting beads, the world will be full of light.

He clearly suggests moral discrimination betwecn good and bad deeds. What can the helpless road do, when the traveller does not walk understandingly. "What can one do, if, with lamp in hand, one falls in the well." "Or goes astray with open eyes.

Discern ye now between good and evil." It is not surprising that Kabir's satire was brought to bear not simply on the vices and weaknesses of men but reached through and beyond them to the very system themselves.

It was the authority of Vedas and Quran that more then the authority of Brahmin or Qazi which Kabir attacked. He rebelled against the pretension of resolving by the means of books or by way of authority, the mystery of human conditions and the problem of liberation (Moksha).

He spent his last 40 days living in a place where it was believed that if you die you will born as a Donkey in next life. Kabir is a firm advocate of ahimsa. His doctrine extends even to the nondestruction of flowers. " The life of the living you strike dead and you say your slaughter makes it dedicated.

It is blood haunting you and those who taught you." "They fast all day, and at night they slaughter the cow; here murder, there devotion; how can this please God? O' Kazi, by whose order doth thou use thy knife." "When you declare the sacrifice of an animal as your religion, what else is sin. If you regard yourself a saint, whom will you call a butcher ?" "The goat eats grass and is skinned, what will happen to those who eat (goat's) meat? "Do not kill poor jiva, murder will not be forgiven even if you hear a million Puranas.

Among the fifty commandments laid down for the followers of Kabir, vegetarianism is one of them. For Kabir, moral life involves adherence to ahimsa. In common with all monastic, ascetic or otherworldly sects, Kabir does not think well of women.

I here is almost a tirade against them in the hymns of Kabir. Woman is characterised as "a black cobra', thc pit of hell and the refuse of the world." She is considered to be a hurdle in the path of thc spiritual progress of man.

He spoke, "woman ruins everything when she comes near a man; Devotion, salvation and divine knowledge no longer enter his soul." His views, about woman are also evident from all his vehement attacks against maya. Almost everywhere he links maya to a woman who is out to entice and entrap man, and destroy his spiritual lifc.

Such views about woman from a married person arc, indeed, quite uncommon. The cosmological views of Kabir give a clear clue to his worldview. He finds Niranjana to be the creator of the world; maya or woman. And this woman stands between man and god.

She is there to entice him away from Him. Kabir composed no systematic treatise, rather his work consists of many short didactic poems, often expressed in terse vigorous language in the form of Padas, Dohas, and Ramainis (forms of poetry in Indian languages).

Besides his work recorded in 1604 A.D. in Guru Granth Sahib by Guru Arjan Dev, Nanak V, and preserved inviolate since, two other collections exist - Kabir Granthavali, and Bijak. In his poems, he was quick to tell the illustrations of moral and spiritual truth in the incidents of everyday life , and many of his similes and metaphors are very striking.

SIDNEY SHELDON

Sidney Sheldon was born on 11th February 1917, in Chicago, USA. After spending six months at Northwestern University during the Depression era, Sheldon dropped out to support his family, making money as a radio joke-writer and a movie house usher, before moving to Hollywood to become a writer, eventually landing a $17 a week job as a script editor, in 1937.

Having spent a year on active service in the US Airforce (1941), Sheldon began writing 'B' movies with collaborator, Ben Roberts. His first screen-writing credit came in 1941, with the film 'Mr. District Attorney' and the 'Carter Case', although it was in scripting musicals that he found his first measure of success. In 1948, Sheldon won an Academy Award for his script to the Cary Grant vehicle, 'The Bachelor and Bobby Soxer', as well as a Screen Writers' Guild Award for Best Musical, for 'Easter Parade', starring Fred Astaire and Judy Garland. In 1953, he made his directorial debut with 'Dream Wife'. However, his efforts as a director and producer rarely matched his accomplishments as a scriptwriter, and later as a novelist.

In 1959 he won a Tony Award for the Best Musical with 'Redhead', as well as becoming an extraordinarily prolific scriptwriter for such shows as 'I Dream of Jeannie' and 'Patty Duke'. Sheldon's first novel, 'The Naked Face', was described by the New York Times as "the best first mystery of the year", and was the first in a seemingly endless production of bestsellers, including 'The Other Side of Midnight' (1974) and 'The Best Laid Plans'(1997).

The octogenarian Sheldon remains active, and is married to Alexandra Kostoff, with whom he has a daughter, Mary. Sheldon holds a Guinness World Record as the most translated single author. His publishers, William Morris, estimate that there are some 275 million copies of his books in circulation across the globe.

SIR ARTHUR CONAN DOYLE

Arthur Conan Doyle was born in Edinburgh, Scotland, in 1859. Doyle's family (Conan was his middle name, and it was only later in life that he began to use it as his surname) sent him to Jesuit boarding schools to be educated, and he later entered the University of Edinburgh Medical School in 1881.

One of his professors at the university was Dr. Joseph Bell, who became the model for Doyle's Sherlock Holmes. It was Bell who drummed into Doyle's head the importance of using his innate powers of observation to help him deduce the nature of a patient's affliction.

While in school, Conan Doyle began writing to earn a little extra money. His first story, *The Mystery of the Sasassa Valley* was published in the Chambers' Journal in 1879.

Shortly after, his father fell ill, and Doyle was forced to become the breadwinner for the family. He worked for a time as a ship's doctor, then opened his own medical practice near Portsmouth. In his spare time he did more writing.

In 1885 Conan Doyle married Louise Hawkins, and had two children with her, before she died after a protracted illness in 1900. In 1907 he remarried, to Jeanne Leckie, and had three more children with her.

His third attempt at a novel was *A Study in Scarlet*, the story which introduced Sherlock Holmes to the world. *Study* was published in Mrs. Beeton's Christmas annual, in 1887. Encouraged by publishers to keep writing, Conan Doyle wrote his second Holmes mystery, *The Sign of the Four*, in 1890.

So successful were these novels, and the stories which followed, that Conan Doyle could afford to give up his medical practice and devote himself to writing full time.

The first Sherlock Holmes short story, *A Scandal in Bohemia*, appeared in The Strand Magazine in 1891, to be followed by two dozen more stories over the next several years.

The stories proved enormously successful, but Conan Doyle tired of his own creation, and in 1894 he killed Holmes off in *The Final Problem*.

He underestimated the popularity of his creation. So great was the hold that the character of Sherlock Holmes had taken on the public imagination that Conan Doyle found himself at the centre of a storm of controversy.

He was inundated with letters of protest, including one from a female reader who addressed him simply as "You Brute!". He bowed to the inevitable, and revived the character of Holmes, who appeared in numerous short stories over the next 23 years.

But Conan Doyle did not confine himself to Sherlock Holmes; he wrote several popular works of historic fiction, including *Micah Clarke (1888), The White Company (1890), Rodney Stone (1896),* and *Sir Nigel (1906).*

Conan Doyle served as a doctor in the Boer War, and on his return he wrote two books defending England's participation in that conflict. It was for these books that he received his knighthood in 1902.

After the death of his son in World War I, Conan Doyle became interested in spiritualism. He was convinced that it was possible to communicate with the dead, and his views led to a certain amount of ridicule from more mainstream society.

Sir Arthur Conan Doyle died on July 7, 1930, and is buried in the churchyard at Minstead Hampshire. He can rightly be credited with helping create the literary genre of the detective story. Though Edgar Allen Poe's Dupin predates Sherlock Holmes, it was the Holmes' stories that solidified in the public mind what a good detective should be.

SIR VIDIADHAR SURAJPRASAD NAIPAUL

English author, Chaguanas, Trinidad; grad. University College, Oxford, 1953. Naipul, whose family is descended from Indian Brahmins, has lived in England since 1950. A master of English prose style, he is known for his penetrating analyses of alienation and exile.

In fiction and essays marked by stylistic virtuosity and psychological insight, he often focuses on his childhood and his travels beyond Trinidad. Writing with increasing irony and pessimism, he has often bleakly detailed the dual problems of the Third World: the oppressions of colonialism and the chaos of postcolonialism.

Among Naipaul's works of international analysis are *The Middle Passage* (1962), about the West Indies and South America, and an Indian trilogy: *An Area of Darkness* (1964), *India: A Wounded Civilization* (1977), and *India: A Million Mutinies Now* (1990).

His novels include *The Mystic Masseur* (1957), *A House for Mr. Biswas* (1961), *In a Free State* (1971; Booker Prize), *Guerrillas* (1975), *A Bend in the River* (1979), and *Half a Life* (2001) and its sequel, *Magic Seeds* (2004); he has also written numerous short stories.

Among his other works are *The Enigma of Arrival* (1987) and *A Way in the World* (1994), autobiographical works combining novel, memoir, and history; *Among the Believers* (1981) and *Beyond Belief* (1998), analyses of modern Islam; and many political essays, a representative sample of which are collected in *The Writer and the World* (2002). Naipaul was knighted in 1990 and awarded the Nobel Prize in Literature in 2001.

THOMAS HARDY

Thomas Hardy was born at Higher Bockhampton, Dorset, on June 2, 1840, where his father worked as a master mason and builder. From his father he gained an appreciation of music, and from his mother an appetite for learning and the delights of the countryside about his rural home.

Hardy was frail as a child, and did not start at the village school until he was eight years old. One year later he transferred to a new school in the county town of Dorchester.

At the age of 16 Hardy helped his father with the architectural drawings for a restoration of Woodsford Castle. The owner, architect James Hicks, was impressed by the younger Hardy's work, and took him on as an apprentice. Hardy later moved to London to work for prominent architect Arthur Blomfield. He began writing, but his poems were rejected by a number of publishers. Although he enjoyed life in London, Hardy's health was poor, and he was forced to return to Dorset.

In 1870 Hardy was sent to plan a church restoration at St. Juliot in Cornwall. There he met Emma Gifford, sister-in-law of the vicar of St.Juliot. She encouraged him in his writing, and they were married in 1874. Hardy published his first novel, *Desperate Remedies* in 1871, to universal disinterest. But the following year *Under the Greenwood Tree* brought Hardy popular acclaim for the first time.

As with most of his fictional works, *Greenwood Tree* incorporated real places around Dorset into the plot, including the village school of Higher Bockhampton that Hardy had first attended as a child. The success of *Greenwood Tree* brought Hardy a commission to write a serialized novel, *A Pair of Blue Eyes*, for Tinsley's Magazine. Once more Hardy drew upon real life, and the novel mirrors his own courtship of Emma.

Hardy followed this with *Far From the Madding Crowd*, set in Puddletown (renamed Weatherby), near his birthplace. This novel finally netted Hardy the success that enabled him to give up his architectural practice and concentrate solely on writing. The Hardys lived in London for a short time, then in Yeovil, then in Sturminster Newton (Stourcastle), which Hardy described as "idyllic". It was at Sturminster Newton that Hardy penned *Return of the Native*, one of his most enduring works.

Finally the Hardys moved to Dorchester, where Thomas designed their new house, Max Gate, into which they moved in 1885. One year later Hardy published *The Mayor of*

Casterbridge, followed in 1887 by *The Woodlanders* and in 1891 by one of his best works, *Tess of the d'Urbervilles. Tess* provoked interest, but his next work, *Jude the Obscure* (1896), catapulted Hardy into the midst of a storm of controversy. *Jude* outraged Victoria morality and was seen as an attack upon the institution of marriage.

Its publication caused a rift between Thomas and Emma, who feared readers would regard it as describing their own marriage.

Of course the publicity did no harm to book sales, but reader's hid the book behind plain brown paper wrappers, and the Bishop of Wakefield burned his copy!

Hardy himself was bemused by the reaction his book caused, and he turned away from writing fiction with some disgust. For the rest of his life Hardy focussed on poetry, producing several collections, including *Wessex Poems* (1898). Emma Hardy died in November 1912, and was buried in Stinsford churchyard.

Thomas was stricken with guilt and remorse, but the result was some of his best poetry, expressing his feelings for his wife of 38 years.

All was not gloom, however, for in 1914 Hardy remarried, to Florence Dugdale, his secretary since 1912. Thomas Hardy died on January 11, 1928 at his house of Max Gate in Dorchester.

He had expressed the wish to be buried beside Emma, but his wishes were only partly regarded; his body was interred in Poet's Corner, Westminster Abbey, and only his heart was buried in Emma's grave at Stinsford.

TULSIDAS

Gosvami Tulsidas (1532-1623) was an Awadhi poet and philosopher. He was born in Rajapur, India in the district of Banda in Uttar Pradesh, during the reign of Humayun. Tulsidas wrote twelve books and is considered the greatest and most famous of Hindi poets. He is regarded as an incarnation of Valmiki, the author of Ramayana written in Sanskrit. He wrote *Ramacaritamanasa* ("The Lake of the Deeds of Rama"), an epic devoted to Lord Rama.

This Awadhi version of Ramayana, like many translations of the original Sanskrit Ramayana, is read and worshipped with great reverence in many Hindu homes in northern India. It is an inspiring book that contains sweet couplets in beautiful rhyme called 'chaupai'. *Vinaya Patrika* is another important book written by Tulsidas. He is considered one of the northern Indian Sants.

Tulsidas is the Prophet of Hinduism and has written the *Ramacaritamanasa*, as dictated by God, which is the new Veda for the Kalyug. This new Veda teaches us that salvation to God can be done, not by sacrifices, rituals, nor intense yoga, but by simple devotion to Ram (God) and by doing good service to every living being. Tulsidas was a Sarayuparina Brahmin by birth. His father's name was Atma Ram Dube; that of his mother is said to have been Hulasi.

A legend relates that, having been born under an unlucky conjunction of the stars, he was abandoned in infancy by his parents, and was adopted by a wandering sadhu or ascetic, with whom he visited many holy places in the length and breadth of India; and the story is in part supported by passages in his poems.

He got his name Tulsi because he devoted a lot of time in looking after the Tulsi plants. He studied, apparently after having rejoined his family, at Sukar-khet, a place generally identified with Soro in the Etah district of the Uttar Pradesh, but more probably the same as Varahakshetra on the Ghagra River, 30 miles west of Ayodhya (Varahakshetra and Sukar-khet have the same meaning; Varaha or Sukara means a wild boar).

He married during his father's lifetime, and begat a son. His wife was Ratnavali, daughter of Dinabandhu Pathak. Their son Tarak died at an early age. Ratnavali, devoted to the worship of Rama, then left her husband and returned to her father's house to occupy herself with religion.

Tulsidas followed her, and endeavoured to induce her to return to him, but in vain; she reproached him (in verses which have been preserved) with want of faith in Rama, and so moved him that he renounced the world, and entered upon an ascetic life, much of which was spent in wandering as a preacher of the necessity of a loving faith in Rama.

He first made Ayodhya his headquarters, frequently visiting distant places of pilgrimage in different parts of India. During his residence at Ayodhya the Lord Rama is said to have appeared to him in a dream, and to have commanded him to write a Ramayana in the language used by the common people.

He began this work in the year 1574, and had finished the third book (Aranyakanda), when differences with the Vairagi Vaishnavas at Ayodhya, to whom he had attached himself, led him to migrate to Benares. Here he died in 1623, during the reign of the emperor Jahangir, at the age of 91.

The period of his greatest activity as an author synchronized with the latter half of the reign of Akbar (1556-1605), and the first portion of that of Jahangir, his dated works being as follows: commencement of the Ramayan, 1574; Ram-satsai, 1584; Parvati-mangal, 1586; Ramajña Prashna, 1598; Kabitta Ramayan, between 1612 and 1614.

A deed of arbitration in his hand, dated 1612, relating to the settlement of a dispute between the sons of a land-owner named Todar, who possessed some villages adjacent to Benares, has been preserved, and is reproduced in facsimile in Dr. Grierson's Modern Vernacular Literature of Hindustan, p. 51. Todar (who was not, as formerly supposed, Akbar's finance minister, the celebrated Raja Todar Mal) was his close friend, and a beautiful and pathetic poem by Tulsi on his death is extant.

He is said to have been resorted to, as a venerated teacher, by Maharaja Man Singh of Jaipur (d. 1618), his brother Jagat Singh, and other powerful princes; and it appears to be certain that his great fame and influence as a religious leader, which remain pre-eminent to this day, were fully established during his lifetime.

Tulsidas's most famous poem is *Ramacaritamanasa*, or "The Lake of the Deeds of Rama". It is popularly called *Tulsi-krita Ramayana* and is as well known among Hindus in North India. Many of its verses are popular proverbs in that region.

Tulsidas' phrases have passed into common speech, and are used by millions of Hindi speakers (and even speakers of Urdu) without the speakers being conscious of their origin. Not only are his sayings proverbial: his doctrine actually forms the most powerful religious influence in present-day Hinduism; and, though he founded no school and was never known as a guru or master, he is everywhere accepted as both poet and saint, an inspired and authoritative guide in religion and the conduct of life.

Tulsidas professed himself the humble follower of his teacher, Narhari-Das, from whom as a boy in Sukar-khet he first heard the tale of Rama's exploits that would form the subject of the *Ramacaritamanasa*. (Narhari-Das was the sixth in spiritual descent from Ramananda, the founder of popular Vaishnavism in northern India.)

Besides the *Ramacaritamanasa*, Tulsidas was the author of five longer and six shorter works, most of them dealing with the theme of Rama, his doings, and devotion to him. The former are the *Dohavali*, consisting of, 573 miscellaneous doha and sortha verses; of this there is a duplicate in the Ram-satsai, an arrangement of seven centuries of verses, the great majority of which occur also in the Dohavali and in other works of Tulsi the *Kabitta Ramayan* or *Kavitavali*, which is a history of Rama in the kavitta, ghanakshari, chaupaï and savaiya metres; like the *Ramacaritamanasa*, it is divided into seven kandas or cantos, and is devoted to setting forth the majestic side of Rama's character the *Gitavali*, also in seven kands, aiming at the illustration of the tender aspect of the Lord's life; the metres are adapted for singing the *Krishnavali* or *Krishna gitavali*, a collection of 61 songs in honor of Krishna, in the Kanauji dialect of Hindi: the authenticity of this is doubtful the *Vinaya Patrika*, or *Book of petitions*, a series of hymns and prayers of which the first 43 are addressed to the lower gods, forming Rama's court and attendants, and the remainder, Nos. 44 to 279, to Rama himself.

Of the smaller compositions the most interesting is the *Vairagya Sandipani*, or *Kindling of continence*, a poem describing the nature and greatness of a holy man, and the true peace to which he attains.

Tulsidas's most famous and read piece of literature apart from the Ramayana is the "Hanuman Chalisa", a poem primarily praising the god Hanuman. Although it is not one of his best poems, it has gained popularity among the modern-day Hindus. Many of them recite it as a prayer every week.

Tulsi's doctrine is derived from Ramanuja through Ramananda. Like the former, he believes in a supreme personal God, possessing all gracious qualities (sadguna), as well as in the quality-less (nirguna) neuter impersonal Brahman of Sankaracharya; this Lord Himself once took the human form, and became incarnate, for the blessing of mankind, as Rama. The body is therefore to be honored, not despised. The Lord is to be approached by faith (bhakti) disinterested devotion and surrender of self in perfect love, and all actions are to be purified of self-interest in contemplation of Him.

Show love to all creatures, and thou wilt be happy; for when thou lovest all things, thou lovest the Lord, for He is all in all.

The soul is from the Lord, and is submitted in this life to the bondage of works (karma); Mankind, in their obstinacy, keep binding themselves in the net of actions, and though they know and hear of the bliss of those who have faith in the Lord, they don't attempt the only means of release.

Works are a spider's thread, up and down which she continually travels, and which is never broken; so works lead a soul downwards to the Earth, and upwards to the Lord. The bliss to which the soul attains, by the extinction of desire, in the supreme home, is not absorption in the Lord, but union with Him in abiding individuality.

This is emancipation (mukti) from the burden of birth and rebirth, and the highest happiness. Tulsi, as a Smarta Brahmin, venerates the whole Hindu pantheon, and is especially careful to give Shiva or Mahadeva, the special deity of the Brahmins, his due, and to point out that there is no inconsistency between devotion to Rama and attachment to Shiva (Ramayana, Lankakanda, Doha 3).

But the practical end of all his writings is to inculcate bhakti addressed to Rama as the great means of salvation and emancipation from the chain of births and deaths, a salvation which is as free and open to men of the lowest caste as to Brahmins.

The literary worth of Tulsidas has been highligthed by Acharya Ram Chandra Shukla in his critical work Hindi Sahitya Ka Itihaas.Acharya Shukla has elaborated Tulsi's Lokmangal as the doctrine for social upliftment which made this great poet immortal and comparable to any other world literateur.

VICTOR HUGO

Victor-Marie Hugo was born in Besançon as the son of Joseph-Léopold-Sigisbert Hugo and Sophie Trébuchet. Hugo's father was an officer in Napoleon's army, an enthusiastic republican and ruthless professional soldier, who loved dangers and adventures. After the marriage of his parents had collapsed, he was raised by his mother.

In 1807 Sophie took her family for two years from Paris to Italy, where Léopold served as a governor of a province near Naples. When General Hugo took charge of three Spanish provinces, Sophie again joined her husband. Sophie's lover, General Victor Lahorie, her husband's former Commandin Officer, was shot in 1812 by a firing-squad for plotting against Napoleon.

From 1815 to 1818 Hugo spend in the Pension Cordier in Paris, but most of the classes of the school were held at the Collège Louis-le Grand. He began in early adolescence to write verse tragedies and poetry, and translated Virgil. At the age of sixteen he noted: "Many a great poet is often / Nothing but a literary giraffe: / How great he seems in front, / How small he is behind!" With his brothers he founded in 1819 a review, the *Conservateur Littéraire*. Inspired by the example of the statesman and author François René Chateaubriand, Hugo published his first collection of poems, *Odes et Poésies Diverses* (1822).

It gained him a royal pension from Louis XVIII. As a novelist Hugo made his debut with *Han d'Islande* (1823), which appeared first anonymously in four pocket-sized volumes. It was translated two years later in English and a Norwegian translation was published in 1831. The style of Sir Walter Scott labelled several of his works, among them *Bug-Jargal* (1826).

In 1822 Hugo married Adèle Foucher (d. 1868), who was the daughter of an officer at the ministry of war. His brother Eugéne, who had mental problems, was secretly in love with her and lost his mind on Hugo's wedding day. Engéne spent the rest of his life in an institution. In the 1820s Hugo come in touch with liberal writers, but his political stand wavered from side to side.

He wrote royalist odes, cursed the memory of Napoleon, but then started to defend his father's role in Napoleon's victories, and attack the injustices of the monarchist regime. General Hugo died in 1828; at that time Hugo started to call himself a baron.

To sise at six, to dine at ten,
To sup at six, to sleep at ten,
Makes a man live for ten times ten.
(Inscription over the door of Hugo's study)

Hugo's foreword for his play *Cromwell* (1827), a manifesto for a new drama, started a debate between French Classicism and Romanticism. However, Hugo was not a rebel, and not directly involved in the campaign against the bourgeois, but he influenced deeply the Romantic movement and the formulation of its values in France. "The Victor I loved is no more," said Alfred de Vigny, "... now he likes to make saucy remarks and is turning into a liberal, which does not suit him..." Hugo gained a wider fame with his play *Hernani* (1830), in which two lovers poison each other, and with his famous historical work *Notre-Dame de Paris*, which became an instant success. Since its appearance in 1831 the story has became part of the popular culture.

The novel, set in 15th century Paris, tells a moving story of a gypsy girl Esmeralda and the deformed, deaf bell-ringer, Quasimodo, who loves her. Esmeralda aroses passion in Claude Frollo, an evil priest, who discovers that she favors Captain Phoebus. Frollo stabs the captain and Esmeralda is accused of the crime. Quasimodo attempts to shelter Esmeralda in the cathedral. Frollo finds her and when Frollo is rejected by Esmeralda, he leaves her to the executioners. In his despair Quasimodo catches the priest, throws him from the cathedral tower, and disappears. Later two skeletons are found in Esmeralda's tomb - that of a hunchback embracing that of a woman.

In the 1830s Hugo published several volumes of lyric poetry, which were inspired by Juliette Drouet (Julienne-Joséphine Gauvain), an actress with whom Hugo had a liaison until her death in 1882. Adéle had an affair with Hugo's friend Charles-Augustin Sainte-Beuve. "Let us not bury our friendship," Hugo wrote to him, but later described him as a man, who 'lifts his loathsome skirt and says, "Admire me!"' Hugo himself was seen by his fans a Gargantuan, larger-than-life character, and rumors spread that he could eat half an ox at a single sitting, fast for three days, and work non-stop for a week.

Hugo's lyrical style was rich, intense and full of powerful sounds and rhythms, and although it followed the bourgeois popular taste of the period it also had bitter personal tones. Hugo's 'Mme Biard poems' - he had an affair with Léonie d'Aunet (Mme Biard's maiden name) in the 1840s - are intensely sexual. According to Verlaine a typical Hugo love poem was "I like you. You yield to me. I love you. - You resist me. Clear off..."

In his later life Hugo became involved in politics as a supporter of the republican form of government. After three unsuccessful attempts, Hugo was elected in 1841 to the Académie Francaise. This triumph was shadowed by the death of Hugo's daughter Léopoldine. She had married Charles Vacquerie in February 1843, and in September she drowned with her husband. In a poem, 'Tomorrow, At Daybreak', written on the fourth anniversary of her death, Hugo depicted his walk to the place where she was buried:

"I shall not look on the gold of evening falling,

Nor on the sails descending distant towards Harfleur,

And when I come, shall lay upon your grave,

A bouquet of green holly and of flowering briar."

It took a decade before Hugo published again books. After he was made a *pair de France* in 1845, he sat in the Upper Chamber among the lords. He also began to work with a new novel, first titled *Jean Tréjean*, then *Les Misères*. Following the 1848 revolution, with the formation of the Second Republic, Hugo was elected to the Constitutional Assembly and to the Legislative Assembly. When workers started to riot, he led soldiers who stormed barricades in brutal assaults.

When the coup d'état by Louis Napoleon (Napoleon III) took place in 1851, Hugo believed his life to be in danger. "Louis-Napoléon is a traitor," he had declared. "He had violated the Constitution!" Hugo fled to Brussels and then to Jersey. When he was expelled from the island, he moved with his family to Guernsey in the English Channel. In a poem, 'Memory of the Night of the Fourth,' focusing on the overthrown of the Second Republic and the death of a young child, killed by bullets, Hugo wrote about the new emperor:

"Ah mother, you don't understand politics.

Monsieur Napoleon, that's his real name,

Is poor and a prince; loves palaces;

Likes to have horses, valets, money

For his gaming, his table, his bedroom,

His hunts, and he maintains

Family, church and society,

Hugo's partly voluntary exile lasted 20 years. During this time he wrote at Hauteville House some his best works, including *Les Châtiments* (1853) and *Les Misérables* (1862), an epic story about social injustice. *Les Châtiments* became one of the most popular forbidden poetry books.

Les Misérables is set in the Parisian underworld. The protagonist, Jean Valjean, is sentenced to prison for 19 years for stealing a loaf of bread. After his release, Valjean plans to rob monseigneur Myriel, a saintlike bishop, but cancels his plan. However, he forfeits his parole by committing a minor crime, and for this crime Valjean is haunted by the police inspector Javert. Valjean eventually reforms and becomes under the name of M. Madeleine a successful businessman, benefactor and mayor of a northern town. To save an innocent man, Valjean gives himself up and is imprisoned in Toulon.

He escapes and adopts Cosette, an illegitimate child of a poor woman, Fantine. Cosette grows up and falls in love with Marius, who is wounded during a revolutionary fight. Valjean rescues Marius by means of a flight through the sewers of Paris. Cosette and Marius marries and Valjean reveals his past. - The story has been filmed several times and made into a musical by the composer Claude-Michel Schönberg and the librettist Alain Boublil, opening in 1980 in Paris. The English version was realised in 1985 and the Broadway version followed two years later.

Like other Romantic writers, Hugo was interested in Spiritism, and he experimented with table-tapping. After a number of fruitless efforts, his table gave him the final title of *Les Misérables*. Among Hugo's most ambitious works was an epic poem, *La Fin de Satan*, a study of Satan's fall and the history of the universe. Satan is presented more complex character than merely the embodiment of the Evil, but when Milton saw in *Paradise Lost* in Satan's revolt tragic, cosmic grandeur, Hugo brings forth the horror elements. The poem was never completed.

Although Napoleon III granted in 1859 an amnesty to all political exiles, Hugo did not take the bite. *Les Misérables* appeared with an international advertising campaign. The book divided critics but masses were enthusiastic. Pope Pius IX added it with *Madame Bovary* and all the novels of Stendhal and Balzac to the Index of Proscribed Books. Hugo's fleeting affairs with maids and country girls inspired his *Les Chansons des Rues et des Bois* (1865). "The creaking of a trestle bed / Is one of the sounds of paradise," he wrote. Hugo's daughter Adèle, whose apathy and unsociability caused him much worries, went after Lieutenant Albert Pinson to Halifax, Nova Scotia, where his regiment was stationed, and followed also him to Barbados. *Les Travailleurs de la Mer* (1866), a story of hypocrisy, love, and suicide, became a bestseller and later two films were made of it.

Adèle Hugo's biography of her husband appeared in 1863; she died in 1868. Political upheavals in France and the proclamation of the Third Republic made Hugo return to France. The unpopular Napoleon III fell from power the Republic was proclaimed. In 1870 Hugo witnessed the siege of Paris. "There is only enough sugar in Paris for ten days," he wrote in his diary on 8 October. "Meat rationing began today." During the period of the Paris Commune of 1871, Hugo lived in Brussels, from where he was expelled for sheltering defeated revolutionaries.

Hugo's attitude to the Commune was ambivalent: "An admirable thing, stupidly compromised by five or six deplorable ringleaders." After a short time refuge in Luxemburg, he returned to Paris and was elected as a senator of Paris in 1876. Sexually he was still active and his maid, Blanche Lavin, was the constant target of his passions, but not the only one. After an exhaustive period with her, Hugo suffered a mild stroke in June 1878. The infuriated Juliette Drouet, his faithful companion form the 1830s, wrote to her nephew: "You must try to track down the creature who has destroyed my happiness.." Hugo died in Paris on May 22, 1885. He was given a national funeral, attended by two million people, and buried in the Panthéon.

WILLIAM MAKEPEACE THACKERAY

William Makepeace Thackeray was born in Calcutta, India, in 1811, son of Richmond Thackeray, an Indian Civil Servant, and his wife Anne (*née* Becher). Just a few years later his father died, his mother remarried, and the shy and retreating young William was sent to England where he would deal with the harsh realities of isolation and bullying at Charterhouse, a private school in London.

He then went on to attend Trinity College, Cambridge, then studied law at the Middle Temple school, but soon after went to Paris to unsuccessfully try his hand at painting. It was in Paris that he met and married Isabella Shawe (1816–1893) in 1836, with whom he would have two surviving daughters, Anne Isabella (b.1837) and Harriet Marian 'Minnie' (b.1840).

Back in England and suffering massive financial losses, Thackeray started writing articles, reviews, essays and sketches as a journalist. Travel articles about France such as his *Paris Sketch Book* (1840) and *The Yellowplush Correspondence* (1841) were among his first efforts appearing in various magazines and journals including *Fraser's*, *Punch*, and *The Times*. He also illustrated many of his own works.

After the birth of Harriet, Isabella started on what was to be, until her death, numerous bouts of depression, an extensive search for a cure, and ultimately a slow spiral to insanity. She would live apart from William, rarely seeing him or her daughters.

Ever the doting father, Thackeray remained close to his daughters all his life. Anne was his secretary for a while and they both lived with him at his house in London before marrying. The disintegration of his marriage however would have a profound effect on his life and be reflected in the characters of his novels, including the loveless marriage between Rachel and Frank Castlewood in *The History of Henry Esmond, Esq.* (1852) and its sequel *The Virginians* (1857).

Haunting the Literary Clubs of London including the Garrick Club, Thackeray also travelled the Mediterranean, *A Journey from Cornhill to Grand Cairo* (1846) the result. *Book of Snobs* (1848) and *Vanity Fair* (1848) followed soon after, but it was not until *The History of Pendennis* (1850), his semi-autobiographical novel that Thackeray's success as a humorist was confirmed. He then embarked on a series of lectures published as *English Humorists of the Eighteenth Century* (1851) and *Four Georges* (1860), based on the Hanoverian Kings, from his tours of the United States in 1852-53 and 1855-56.

In 1860 Thackeray became editor of the monthly literary journal *Cornhill Magazine*, but died suddenly three years later, in 1863, at the age of fifty two. He lies buried beside his mother in the Victorian Garden cemetery Kensal Green in London, England. Charles Dickens wrote a glowing tribute to him in *Cornhill Magazine*.

Other titles include;
The Luck of Barry Lyndon (1844),
Newcomes (1853),
The Memoirs of Barry Lyndon, Esq. (1856),
Lovel the Widower (1860),
The Adventures of Philip (1860-62), and
Denis Duval (1864).

WILLIAM SHAKESPEARE

Details about William Shakespeares life are sketchy, mostly mere surmise based upon court or other clerical records. His parents, John and Mary (Arden), were married about 1557; she was of the landed gentry, he a yeomana glover and commodities merchant. By 1568, John had risen through the ranks of town government and held the position of high bailiff, similar to mayor.

William, the eldest son, was born in 1564, probably on April 23, several days before his baptism on April 26, 1564. That Shakespeare also died on April 23, 52 years later, may have resulted in the adoption of this birthdate.

William no doubt attended the local grammar school in Stratford where his parents lived, and would have studied primarily Latin rhetoric, logic, and literature. At age 18 (1582), William married Anne Hathaway, a local farmers daughter eight years his senior. Their first daughter (Susanna) was born six months later (1583), and twins Judith and Hamnet were born in 1585.

Shakespeares life can be divided into three periods: the first 20 years in Stratford, which include his schooling, early marriage, and fatherhood; the next 25 years as an actor and playwright in London; and the last five in retirement back in Stratford where he enjoyed moderate wealth gained from his theatrical successes.

The years linking the first two periods are marked by a lack of information about Shakespeare, and are often referred to as the dark years; the transition from active work into retirement was gradual and cannot be precisely dated.

John Shakespeare had suffered financial reverses from Williams teen years until well into the height of the playwrights popularity and success. In 1596, John Shakespeare was granted a coat of arms, almost certainly purchased by William, who the next year bought a sizable house in Stratford. By the time of his death, William had substantial properties, both professional and personal, which he bestowed on his theatrical associates and his family (primarily his daughter Susanna, having rewritten his will one month before his death to protect his assets from Judiths new husband, Thomas Quiney, who ran afoul of church doctrine and public esteem before and after the marriage).

Shakespeare probably left school at 15, which was the norm, and took some sort of job, especially since this was the period of his fathers financial difficulty. Numerous references in his plays suggest that William may have in fact worked for his father, thereby gaining specialized knowledge.

At some point during the dark years, Shakespeare began his career with a London theatrical companyperhaps in 1589for he was already an actor and playwright of some note in 1592. Shakespeare apparently wrote and acted for Pembrokes Men, as well as numerous others, in particular Stranges Men, which later became the Chamberlains Men, with whom he remained for the rest of his career.

When, in 1592, the Plague closed the theaters for about two years, Shakespeare turned to writing book-length narrative poetry. Most notable were Venus and Adonis and The Rape of Lucrece, both of which were dedicated to the Earl of Southampton, whom scholars accept as Shakespeares friend and benefactor despite a lack of documentation. During this same period, Shakespeare was writing his sonnets, which are more likely signs of the times fashion rather than actual love poems detailing any particular relationship. He returned to play writing when theaters reopened in 1594, and published no more poetry. His sonnets were published without his consent in 1609, shortly before his retirement.

Amid all of his success, Shakespeare suffered the loss of his only son, Hamnet, who died in 1596 at the age of 11. But Shakespeares career continued unabated, and in London in 1599, he became one of the partners in the new Globe Theater [Boyce, 589], built by the Chamberlains Men. This group was a remarkable assemblage of excellent actors who were also business partners and close personal friends . . . Richard Burbage . . . [who] all worked together as equals . . . .

When Queen Elizabeth died in 1603 and was succeeded by her cousin King James of Scotland, the Chamberlains Men was renamed the Kings Men, and Shakespeares productivity and popularity continued uninterrupted. He invested in London real estate and, one year away from retirement, purchased a second theater, the Blackfriars Gatehouse, in partnership with his fellow actors. His final play was Henry VIII, two years before his death in 1616.

Incredibly, most of Shakespeares plays had never been published in anything except pamphlet form, and were simply extant as acting scripts stored at the Globe. Only the efforts of two of Shakespeares company, John Heminges and Henry Condell, preserved his 36 plays (minus Pericles, the thirty-seventh) [Barnet, xvii] in the First Folio.

Heminges and Condell published the plays, they said, only to keep the memory of so worthy a friend and fellow alive as was our Shakespeare.

Theater scripts were not regarded as literary works of art, but only the basis for the performance. Plays were a popular form of entertainment for all layers of society in Shakespeares time, which perhaps explains why Hamlet feels compelled to instruct the traveling Players on the fine points of acting, urging them not to split the ears of the groundlings, nor speak no more than is set down for them.

Present copies of Shakespeares plays have, in some cases, been reconstructed in part from scripts written down by various members of an acting company who performed particular roles. Shakespeares plays, like those of many of the actors who also were playwrights, belonged to the acting company. The performance, rather than the script, was what concerned the author, for that was how his play would become popularand how the company, in which many actors were shareholders, would make money.

William Shakespeare died on April 23, 1616, and was buried two days later in the chancel of Holy Trinity Church where he had been baptized exactly 52 years earlier.

WILLIAM SOMERSET MAUGHAM

W. Somerset Maugham was born in Paris as the sixth and youngest son of the solicitor to the British embassy. He learned French as his native tongue.

At the age of 10 Maugham was orphaned and sent to England to live with his uncle, the vicar of Whitstable. Educated at King's School, Canterbury, and Heidelberg University, Maugham then studied six years medicine in London. He qualified in 1897 as doctor from St. Thomas' medical school but abandoned medicine after the success of his first novels and plays.

Maugham lived in Paris for ten years as a struggling young author. In 1897 appeared his first novel, *Liza of Lambeth*, which drew on his experiences of attending women in childbirth. His first play, *A Man of Honour*, was produced in 1903. Four of his plays ran simultaneously in London in 1904. Maugham's breakthrough novel was the semi-autobiographical *Of Human Bondage* (1915), which is usually considered his outstanding achievement.

The story follows the childhood, youth, and early manhood of Philip Carey, who is born with a clubfoot. Philip never knew his father and his mother only for a brief space. He is raised by a religious aunt and uncle, but the real process of his education, after the end of an unsatisfactory social life, begins in Heidelberg. Philip goes to Paris to study art, and at the age of thirty he qualifies as a doctor. Finally he marries Sally Athelny, a normal, healthy, happy girl.

Disguising as a reporter, Maugham worked for British Intelligence in Russia during the Russian Revolution in 1917, but his stuttering and poor health hindered his career in this field. He then set off with a friend on a series of travels to eastern Asia, the Pacific Islands, and Mexico. His most famous story, which became the play *Rain* and was made into several movies, was inspired by a missionary and prostitute among his fellow passengers on a trip to Pago Pago. In the 1928 he settled in Cape Ferrat in France.

His plays, among them *The Circle* (1921), a satire of social life, *Our Betters* (1923), about Americans in Europe, and *The Constant Wife* (1927), about a wife who takes revenge on her unfaithful husband, were performed in Europe and in the United States. Maugham's famous novel *The Moon and the Sixpence* (1919) was the story of Charles Strickland (or actually Paul Gauguin), an artist, whose rejection of Western civilization led to his departure for Tahiti. There he is blinded by leprosy but continues painting. *Trembling of a Leaf* (1921) included the story 'Rain,' made into a play by John Colton and Clemence Randolph in 1922. *Razors Edge* (1944), about a spiritual quest, was made into film two times. "This book consists of my recollections of a man with whom I was thrown into close contact only at long intervals, and I have little knowledge of what happened to him in between," Maugham wrote in the beginning of the story. "I have invented nothing." Maugham tells of a young American veteran who moves through superbly described settings: Italy, London, the Riviera, Montparnasse. He seeks in the end relief in India from the horrors of war and gains a sense of being at one with the Absolute, through the Indian philosophical system known as Vedanta.

As an agent and writer Maugham was a link in a long tradition from Christopher Marlowe, Ben Johnson and Daniel Defoe to the modern day writers Graham Greene, John Le Carré, John Dickson Carr, Alec Waugh and Ted Allbeury. It is said that the modern spy story began with Maugham's *Ashenden; or the British Agent* (1928). It was partly based on the author's own experiences in the secret service. Alfred Hitchcock used in his film *Secret Agent* (1936) specifically the stories 'The Traitor' and 'The Hairless Mexican'. In the film, set in Switzerland, agents kill a wrong man and then they go to after the right one. A chocolate factory is used by the crooks' as a headquarters.

Maugham believed that there is a true harmony in the contradictions of mankind and that the the normal is in reality the abnormal. "The ordinary is the writer's richest field", he stated in *The Summing Up* (1938). In his satirical short story 'The Ant and the Grasshopper' he juxtaposed two brothers, the unscrupulous and carefree Tom and the hardworking, respectable George, who expects that Tom would end in the gutter. However, Tom marries a rich old woman, she dies and leaves him a fortune. "I burst into a shout of laughter as I looked at George's wrathful face.

I rolled in my chair, I very nearly fell in the floor. George never forgave me. But Tom often asks me to excellent dinners in his charming house in Mayfair, and he occasionally borrows a trifle from me, that is merely from force of habit." Although he became world famous he was never knighted and his relationship with Gerald Haxton, his secretary, have been subject to speculations. Maugham died in Nice on December 16, 1965. It is said that as he lay dying he asked Sir Alfred Ayer visit him and reassure him that there was no life after death.

A number of Maugham's short stories have been filmed. *Quartet* (1948) consisted of four stories introduced by the author - 'The Facts of Life', 'The Alien Corn', 'The Kite', and 'The Colonel's Lady.' In 'The Kite' the protagonist, Herbert, starts to fly kites with his parents in childhood. After marriage Herbert continues his hobby, although Betty, his wife, considers it childish. When Herbert wants to buy a new kite, Betty packs his bag and Herbert returns to his parents' house. Betty smashes the kite. The magistrate orders him to pay Betty alimony, twenty-five shillings a week, but Herbert don't obey the order and chooses the prison. "It may be that in some queer way he identifies himself with the kite flying so free and so high above him, and it's as it were an escape from the monotony of life. It may be that in some dim, confused way it represents an ideal of freedom and adventure, And you know, when a man once gets bitten with the virus of the ideal not all the King's doctors and not all the King's surgeons can rid him of it."

"Most people cannot see anything, but I can se what is in front of my nose with extreme clearness; the greatest writers can see through a brick wall. My vision is not so penetrating."

After the 1930s Maugham's reputation abroad was greater than in England. Interest in him revived again in his 80th birthday, which he celebrated by the special republication of *Cakes and Ale* (1930), a novel satirizing London literary circles and 'Grand Old Men'. Among the characters are Maugham as Ashenden, Thomas Hardy as Driffield, and Hugh Walpole as Kear. Barbara Belford listed in *Violet: The Story of the Irrepressible Violet Hunt and Her Circle of Lovers and Friends* (1990) Maugham among the lovers of Violet Hunt with such names as H. G. Wells and Ford Madox Ford.

The novelist Hugh Walpole portrayed Maugham as the arrogant pessimist in *John Cornelius* (1937), he appeared as John-Blair-Kennedy in Noel Coward's *South Sea Bubble* (1956), Leverson Hurle in *Gin and Bitters* by A Riposte, the homosexual novelist in Noel Coward's *Point Valaine* (1935), Kenneth Marchal Toomey in Anthony Burgess *Earthly Powers* (1980), Willie Tower in S.N. Behrman's *Jane* (1946), and Gilbert Hereford Vaughn in Ada Leverson's The Limit (1911). Maugham collected his literary experiences in *The Summing Up*, which has been used as a guidebook for creative writing.

WILLIAM WORDSWORTH

William Wordsworth was born on April 7, 1770, in Cockermouth, Cumberland. His father, John, was a lawyer, and he encouraged his 5 children to pursue learning. When Wordsworth's mother Anne died in 1778, young William was sent to attend grammar school away from home.

Wordsworth's father did not survive his wife by long, and when he died in 1783 the Wordsworth children found themselves living with two uncles who were not best pleased to receive them.

William was sent to Cambridge, and upon graduation he graveled in Europe for a time, but when the money ran out Wordsworth returned home. He published two poems, *Descriptive Sketches*, and *An Evening Walk*, which were not well received. However, friends arranged for money to allow him to concentrate on his writing.

At this time Wordsworth met poet Samuel Taylor Coleridge, and the two became firm friends. They collaborated on a volume of Romantic verse called *Lyrical Ballads* (1798), which was notable for its attempt to use ordinary language in a poetic fashion. Later, Coleridge's drug addiction and erratic behavior put an end to their friendship.

In 1802 Wordsworth received money owed to his father, and he was financially secure enough to marry Mary Hutchinson, an old childhood friend. Mary, William, and his sister Dorothy lived together in the Lake District village of Grasmere.

William published a two-volume set of his poetry in 1807, and once more it was met by public indifference and scathing reviews (by Lord Byron among others).

Wordsworth's happy home life turned to tragedy when two of his four children died within a year.

Shortly thereafter Wordsworth got himself appointed Distributor of Stamps for Westmorland, which brought him enough money to continue writing. Although his poems were critically panned, they were gaining a wide popular readership.

In the absence of success for his poems, Wordsworth turned to travel writing. He published a travel guide to the Lake District which proved very popular.

When Robert Southey, the Poet Laureate, died in 1843, Wordswoth was asked to take his place. He initially refused, pleading his advancing age, but was induced by Sir Robert Peel to take the post. He was still Poet Laureate when he died of pleurisy in 1850.

~~~
~~~